Praise for Heather MacAllister...

"For a good time, read Heather!"
—*New York Times* bestselling author
Christina Dodd

"Curling up with a Heather MacAllister romance is one of my favorite indulgences."
—*New York Times* bestselling author
Debbie Macomber

"*Never Say Never* was an absolutely adorable book. It was funny and sweet.... Great job, Ms. MacAllister."
—*Fallen Angel Reviews*

"Funny, sexy and tantalizing, *Never Say Never* is a tale not to miss, and will chase away any blues you might have."
—*Romance Reviews Today*

"Ms. MacAllister does a splendid job of creating a sexy and sweet romance."
—*A Romance Review*

Dear Reader,

As the song says, "I'm proud to be an Americaaaaan..." A Harlequin American Romance writer, that is. When I first started reading the line, I discovered that the books are fast paced *and* heartwarming—just the type of story I love to write. So to me, it seemed a perfect fit!

I had a lot of fun writing *Lone Star Santa*. First of all, I should mention that Sugar Land, Texas, is a real place. I don't live there, but I live close enough to take advantage of the excellent shopping (heartwarming, at least for me). I love Christmas lights, and the Sugar Land neighborhoods are known for going all out with their displays. However, they don't have a Christmas Light Parade or an outdoor display in Town Square. But I think they should, so I gave them one in this story (even though it would interfere with the aforementioned excellent shopping).

Kristen and Mitch are typical of my heroines and heroes who always try to do the right thing and get tangled up in their good intentions. And while they're untangling themselves, they can't help falling in love. I could draw parallels with tangled strings of Christmas lights, couldn't I?

But you're not looking for parallels; you're looking for a fast-paced, heartwarming story about the pursuit of love in America. You've found it! Start reading.

Best wishes, and happy holidays,

Heather MacAllister

Heather MacAllister

Lone Star Santa

TORONTO • NEW YORK • LONDON
AMSTERDAM • PARIS • SYDNEY • HAMBURG
STOCKHOLM • ATHENS • TOKYO • MILAN • MADRID
PRAGUE • WARSAW • BUDAPEST • AUCKLAND

ISBN-13: 978-0-373-75142-6
ISBN-10: 0-373-75142-7

LONE STAR SANTA

This edition published by arrangement with Harlequin Books S.A.

www.eHarlequin.com

Printed in U.S.A.

ABOUT THE AUTHOR

Heather MacAllister lives near the Texas gulf coast where, in spite of the ten-month growing season and plenty of humidity, she can't grow plants. She's a former music teacher who married her high school sweetheart on the Fourth of July, so is it any surprise that their two sons turned out to be a couple of firecrackers? When she's not writing stories in which life takes a funny twist, Heather collects vintage costume jewelry and loves fireworks displays, Christmas lights (which look like frozen fireworks displays to her), commercial-free television and sons who answer their mother's e-mail. Please visit her Web site at www.heathermacallister.com.

Books by Heather MacAllister

HARLEQUIN TEMPTATION

785—MOONLIGHTING
817—PERSONAL RELATIONS
864—TEMPTED IN TEXAS
892—SKIRTING THE ISSUE
928—MALE CALL
959—HOW TO BE THE PERFECT GIRLFRIEND
981—CAN'T BUY ME LOVE
1014—FALLING FOR YOU
1025—NEVER SAY NEVER

For Collin and Meredith
Long life and much happiness

Chapter One

"I told you Kristie Kringle sounded like a stripper."

"So you thought you'd send me out as one?" Kristen Kringle, née Zaleski, stood on a Los Angeles sidewalk outside the Samurai Salsa Burlesque club as she spoke to her agent. A chili pepper in a kimono posed seductively on the sign.

"Not a stripper, Kristen. Burlesque. It's hot right now. Very family oriented."

"Hot! Raw! Girls! doesn't quite have that Disney ring."

"The hot and the raw means the salsa and the sushi!"

"I know what it means." Kristen checked the time on her call. She was low on prepaid cell phone minutes and didn't want to recharge before the end of the month. Couldn't afford to recharge before the end of the month.

Maybe not even then.

"You said 'Leonard, send me out on anything you've got.' This is what I've got," her agent complained.

"Nothing else?"

"It's a slow time of year. The holidays are coming up, you know."

Kristen knew that, though nobody was dreaming of a white Christmas in Los Angeles. Tofu turkey, maybe.

She eyed the blinking chili pepper. "This isn't exactly an acting job, Len."

"For you it would be," he retorted.

"I beg your pardon!"

"Now that's what I'm talking about. You've got that classy thing going. It comes with the smaller boobs. To be honest, when I saw your head shot and that you were the Sugar Queen—"

"Miss Sweetest of Sugar Land."

"Whatever. The thing is, most Texas beauty queens… well, I was expecting more artificial sweetener, if you get my drift."

"You're mistaking me for Miss Silicon Valley." Still, with judicious use of tape Kristen could fake it. Had faked it. And had suffered with a red rashy tape mark, too.

No. This wasn't what she'd envisioned when she'd headed out to Los Angeles with her bright and shiny Miss Sweetest crown over six years ago.

"Now if you could find a Sugar Daddy…" Len interrupted himself laughing at his own joke, such as it was.

Kristen rolled her eyes. She'd heard them all before. Several times. "No, Len."

"I knew that. Now hon, here's what I'm thinking. You take this gig and pick up some moves from the other gals and you'll prove that your lumps are as good as anybody's. Lumps—get it?"

"Yeah. I get it."

"It's all about perception."

Kristen studied her cleavage. It was there. Somewhere. "I thought it was all about boobs."

"See, that's what I like about you. You still have your sense of humor."

But not her car, which was currently transmissionless. "What about commercials? The orange juice people seemed happy with my work." Her legs were good, if she could just get people to look down. "Maybe I can be a tomato or something."

"A tomato—ha!"

Kristen didn't understand what was so funny. "Or how about the department stores? Don't they need demonstrators this time of year? You know, Len, nobody sprays perfume like I do." That sounded too desperate. Well, she was desperate.

To her surprise, Len abandoned his attempt to talk her into the ethnically confused burlesque show. "Hon, I know you've got talent. You know you've got talent. It's the casting people we've got trouble with. I still think the smart Texas beauty queen hook works, but in Los Angeles, not so much. You're more stage. Think east. Think New York."

Kristen flashed back to drama classes. Stage acting was all very well and good, but for real fame, it was TV or movies. Youth wasn't so important on the stage. But with high-definition television exposing every little imperfection, youth definitely ruled. Kristen had thought she was being practical going for film work now, if maxing out her credit cards and taking survival temp jobs could be considered being practical.

But after six years, it had come to this: Spraying

perfume at people, sweating inside gigantic fruit costumes and Hot! Raw! Girls!

And, frankly, the first blush of youth had faded.

Leonard was still talking. "I have an agreement with a New York agency—a buddy of mine. We send each other talent. I could give him a call."

Honestly, Leonard was being far nicer than she'd expected when she'd refused this job. He was dumping her, she'd figured that out, but he was dumping her in a face-saving way she appreciated. She didn't blame him. She'd been picky lately, and he'd never made much money off her.

Truthfully, she was discouraged. Ever since she'd dropped out of the University of Texas at twenty and headed for Los Angeles, she'd supported herself doing office temp work. She told people she was an actress, and it was true that she was always acting. She acted enthusiastic, she acted as though she loved auditions and she acted as though she hadn't maxed out her credit cards. But now she was having a moment of truth. And truthfully, she was an office temp. An office temp with not-so-great typing skills who hadn't kept up with the latest software, but that's how she made her living, such as it was. It had taken a red-and-green blinking, kimono-dressed chili pepper to make her see it.

"Tell you what, Len. I do appreciate the offer. And New York is…well, New York. But I haven't seen my parents for a long time. I think I'm just going to head home for the holidays and decide what to do."

"You do that, sweetie. Sweetie, get it?" He gave a bark of laughter. "Listen, I got another call. Keep in touch."

He ended the call and that was that.

Well, not quite that. There was her car to deal with. A car was a basic necessity in Los Angeles. As it was in Texas, for that matter. Currently, fourteen-hundred dollars stood between Kristen and a running automobile.

Okay. Time to regroup.

Though she'd just blurted out the bit about going home, now that she thought about it, that was her best option.

She walked down the cracked sidewalk around to the back of the strip of buildings where she'd been told to park. She had a rental car and was relieved to discover that it was still there and apparently still possessed all its parts and tires.

She unlocked the car, got inside and locked the door again. And then she sat.

This car was bottom of the line and the cheapest rental available. It only had eight thousand miles on it and had been liberally sprayed with new car smell. She'd enjoyed driving it the past three days. Enjoyed knowing that when she turned the key, it would start, and once started, it would continue to run until she decided it should stop. And the working radio was nice, too. Little luxuries she'd done without for a long time.

Kristen leaned her head back against the neck rest and inhaled.

She'd become a cliché and she'd promised herself that she'd never become a cliché, but if a small-town beauty queen getting chewed up and spit out by Hollywood wasn't a cliché, then what was it?

She hadn't even wanted to enter the stupid pageant. It had been a joke to prove that only blondes became Miss Sweetest and she was definitely a brunette. Only, she'd been accepted. And then she'd made the semifinals and then her competitive spirit had kicked in and then there were the finals and the questions and, well, Kristen had been on the debate team.

She'd blown the blondes out of the water. She'd looked mighty good in that crown. It had been a great year. She'd been given a newspaper column in which she'd written about her experiences, and had logged more personal appearances than any other Miss Sweetest. By the time her reign ended, she'd become poised and polished. Opportunity knocked. Doors opened. Acting invitations arrived and she'd accepted them and now here she was…sitting in the parking lot of a burlesque house.

Yeah, way to go Kristen.

She'd never failed at anything in her life. No, she'd failed *at* life.

Ooo, wasn't she having a lovely pity party?

Okay, enough of that. She wasn't a failure; she just wasn't a success yet. Still, home was looking pretty good right now. She hadn't been home since her little sister's wedding and that had hardly been the home she remembered. It had been Wedding Central.

Kristen smiled to herself. Her parents must be bored out of their minds now that Kristen and Nicole weren't living there. They probably spent all their time eating frozen dinners and flipping back and forth between the weather channel and the home shopping channel. Oh, and the old black-and-white movies they watched together. Just how many black-and-white film noirs had been made, anyway?

She should have come home more often. They

would be thrilled to see her. She had a responsibility to check up on them. She shouldn't have left their well-being all to Nicole. Nicole didn't even live in Sugar Land anymore.

Her poor parents were just sitting in front of the TV waiting for the grandchildren to appear.

Kristen had to go rescue them from a life of drudgery.

While she was rescuing them, she'd live at home and save rent money. She could borrow a car, too, because she'd just made up her mind to sell her old car for scrap. She'd settle up with the rent, repay everybody she'd borrowed from, make a token payment on her credit card and head for home. She happened to know that a one-way bus ticket from Los Angeles to her home was less than a hundred and twenty-five dollars.

Before she could change her mind, Kristen punched the speed dial on her phone.

"Hey Mom!"

"Kristen? *Kristen?* What's wrong?"

Why did her mother always assume something was wrong? "Everything's fine. I—"

"Can you hold? I'm on the other line."

What other line? "I don't really have enough minutes to hold. I just wanted—"

"Then I'll call you right back. I need to deal with this other call, and then I want to hear your news."

Oh, great. Her mother probably thought she'd finally gotten her big break. Or little break. Or any break.

Kristen used the time she waited for her mother to call her back to loosen her mouth and practice injecting enthusiasm into her voice.

The phone rang. "Now tell me everything," her mother said.

Kristen pasted a wide smile on her face. People could hear smiles. "I'm coming home for the holidays!"

A beat went by. "You are?"

"Yes!" Kristen felt herself relax as she envisioned her mother's expression of delighted surprise.

"Why?"

"What do you mean, why?" She laughed. "It's the holidays. Going home for the holidays is what people *do*." Kristen couldn't remember the last Thanksgiving she'd spent at home, but never mind. She was going to make up for it now.

"Which holidays?" her mother asked.

"Why…all of them!" There was silence. Her mother was obviously stunned with happiness. "Oh, Mom, it'll be great. I know I haven't been home much lately—"

"Not since your sister's wedding two years ago."

Had it been *two* years? "That long?"

"That long."

Okay, so her mother was understandably cautious about giving free rein to her happiness. "Well, that changes now. You can start decking the halls and killing the fatted calf because I promise that Kristen Kringle is coming home."

"Who?"

"Me, Mom."

Her mother snorted. "I'm sorry! It's just…it sounds like a stripper's name!"

"So I've been told." Kristen watched the reflection of the blinking chili pepper in the windows of the building across the street. "Anyway, I'll see you in a couple of days, Mom. It'll be good to come home."

MITCH DONNER had overslept and still only managed about five hours sleep. If anybody deserved a double shot latte this morning, he did. So, yeah, he indulged himself. He was already late and the downtown Dallas traffic made him even later. But it was weird the way people glanced at him and looked away as he got off the elevator. It wasn't as though he did this a lot. And even if he did, so what? Owning half the company ought to be good for *some* perks.

"Hey, it's only ten after nine," he muttered when Lindsey, the receptionist, barely managed to return his greeting. He didn't add that he'd been here all weekend working by himself. That revealed more about the current state of his social life than he wanted known.

Social life. He thought for a moment. "Did I miss somebody's birthday party this weekend? Wedding?"

"No, sir," Lindsey said without looking at him and pressed a button on the console.

Sir? Since when had he become a "sir"?

"Sloane and Donner Financial Services. How may I direct your call?"

"Donner and Sloane" sounded better, but it mattered to Jeremy to have his name first and he was the more visible partner while Mitch was the work-on-the-weekends partner.

And apparently the stepped-in-something-smelly partner, too. As Lindsey pressed another button, Mitch gestured for the interoffice mail. There wasn't any yet, so he sipped his coffee and headed toward his office.

He heard voices and saw a couple of men hanging around outside his door.

What now? Clearly, it was going to be one of those days. He stopped walking, chugged the rest of his coffee and hoped the caffeine would kick in pronto.

And then one of the men standing outside his office turned and Mitch saw SEC emblazoned in yellow on the back of his windbreaker and the issue of caffeine became moot, what with the adrenaline spurt.

What were the Securities and Exchange guys doing here?

These were the field guys. The guys who seized files and computers and stuff. Apparently Mitch's stuff. This could not be good.

Where was Jeremy? Mitch tried for a cautious, yet confident, demeanor as he approached the men. It wasn't as though he'd done anything wrong, or even close to wrong, a stance that frequently put him at odds with Jeremy, his partner in Sloane and Donner Financial Services. Jeremy was a little too creative with money but Mitch was a little too careful, so together, they were about perfect.

He reached his office door and looked in. It was worse than he'd thought.

"Mitch, buddy." Jeremy stepped over to him and took his arm—the one not holding a briefcase. The arm holding a briefcase was liberated of said briefcase by one of the SEC men.

"What's going on?" Mitch kept his voice low and calm. In retrospect, it might have been better if he'd shouted.

"Buddy—why didn't you tell me you were in trouble?" Jeremy wore his concerned sympathy face—

the face he wore when he faced clients who'd followed their advice and yet, inexplicably, lost money.

Mitch's eyes narrowed. Jeremy had taught him that face. He'd practiced it with him. Mitch was not fooled by that face. Jeremy was worried. "What do you mean 'trouble'?"

Jeremy gestured as two men wheeled out his file cabinet on a dolly. "You're over an hour late. I could have used a heads up." Jeremy managed to speak without moving his lips.

"I overslept! You know I spent all weekend here and—"

"I'd keep that to myself for now." Jeremy glanced at one of the men—the one who wasn't wearing a windbreaker with SEC on it, but was talking into a cell phone. He stared at them.

Mitch knew why he stared at them—Jeremy looked guilty. In fact, Jeremy couldn't have looked guiltier if he'd held a blinking sign over his head.

"You look guilty," he told him.

"No, Mitch. I look concerned, but cooperative." His grip tightened.

Mitch pulled his arm away. "What are we cooperating with? What's going on? What do they think is wrong?"

"Well, Mitch, that's what we're trying to find out." Glancing over at the man again, he leaned closer to Mitch. "I'll handle this. Just play along."

"It would help if I knew the game!"

"The game is stay out of jail, buddy."

Mitch couldn't think of anything to say. He simply couldn't process what was happening. He'd always followed the rules. Prided himself on doing so, even.

Nothing he'd done recently, or in the past few weeks—or ever—was even remotely suspicious.

He drew a breath to ask if Jeremy knew what they were supposed to have done, but Jeremy rubbed the place above his eyebrow. The "be quiet" signal.

So Mitch swallowed his questions and leaned against his office wall. Way back when they were in business school together, heck, even before that when they'd been in high school in Sugar Land, Texas, Mitch had learned that Jeremy was very good at reading people and good things always happened when Mitch stood back and let Jeremy take over. This method had worked for them in the eight years since they'd gone into partnership with each other and Mitch sure hoped it worked now.

He watched as the men packed up his computer, every pencil, pen and paper clip in his desk and even his office plant. Some palm thing. "They're taking my plant." He turned to Jeremy in genuine bewilderment. "Did they take all your stuff?"

Jeremy looked at his shoes in much the same way everybody in the outer office had found the carpeting so fascinating this morning.

"You're kidding," Mitch said flatly. "Just my stuff?"

Drawing a deep breath, Jeremy met his eyes. "I don't care what you've done. I'm here for you. And we'll get you a good lawyer. The best."

"I don't need a lawyer!"

"I'm thinking you do." The head-honcho type approached them and handed Mitch a card.

Mitch blinked, his vision as fuzzy as his brain, barely able to make out "FBI Economic Crimes Unit." FBI?

The FBI was here, too? Crimes? This could not be happening, at least not to him. "There's got to be some mistake," he said to the man. He squinted at the card. "Mr. Jenkins."

"Then we'll find it."

"I—" He couldn't think of a thing to say. It was as though someone had filled his head with molasses. Not enough sleep.

He'd been working such long hours because it was nearing the end of the year and many of their clients made adjustments to their financial portfolios at this time for tax purposes. Nothing unusual. It was always this way. And the truth was, he liked the work. It meant business was good. It meant end-of-the-year profits.

He waved his hand around his denuded office. "What am I supposed to do? Our clients—"

"Don't worry," Jeremy broke in. "Go home. Take the rest of the day off. In fact take a couple of days. The rest of the week."

"You might give us a few hours before you head back home." Jenkins smiled without mirth. "Do some early Christmas shopping." He handed Mitch a piece of paper. "You can make one ATM withdrawal."

Several beats passed before Mitch understood that Jenkins' men were in his town house, presumably leaving it in the same condition as his office.

No.

He turned, but Jenkins stopped him. "You'll have to sign the paper."

"What is this?"

"Basically, it says we've impounded the contents of your office until such time as we evaluate the evidence."

The words swam before his eyes. "What if I don't sign?"

Jenkins shrugged. "Stuff tends to get lost."

Right. Mitch signed, aware that Jeremy had been remarkably quiet during everything. He was no doubt as shocked as Mitch was.

Mitch handed Jenkins his precious paper and promptly took his own shocked self back home.

BAD MOVE. OUTSIDE HIS town house, Mitch leaned against his car, which he'd parked at the curb because, hey, he didn't want to block the truck into which SEC minions were loading his possessions.

And, oh, it wasn't his own personal car. It was a rental because his own personal car had been impounded.

As soon as he got his breathing under control—getting just the right speed to avoid hyperventilation was tricky at the moment—he'd give Jeremy a call. Just a, "Hey, how's it goin'? What the hell is going on?" call.

He gripped the cell phone and held his breath. It beat breathing into a paper bag.

He speed dialed Jeremy.

Jeremy answered with, "This isn't a good time for me."

"Well, *buddy*, this isn't such a hot time for me, either." Mitch spoke through clenched teeth. He hoped anyone watching would think was a smile. "A Jenkins clone is here with his minions. They're taking 'items of interest.' Then I'll be allowed to pack. Then, they're sealing off my town house and I won't be able to get back into it for God knows how long. They don't seem to care where I go—maybe because they've made it so hard for me to go anywhere. Did I mention they took my car? I had to rent one. I used the corporate card, since all my freaking credit cards are frozen."

"I have no idea what they're looking for," Jeremy said in a barely audible voice. "You know with all the corporate malfeasance of the past few years the Feds are probably being extra careful."

"Whatever." Mitch was suddenly very, very tired. "Maybe we can figure it out tonight. Obviously, I need a place to crash. After Jenkins II is finished here, I'll come by the office and get your key, unless you've got an extra floating around somewhere outside your place."

A couple of beats went by. "That doesn't work for me."

Mitch blinked. "It doesn't work for me, either, but I've got nowhere else to go and the three hundred bucks I got out of the ATM isn't going to last me too long."

There was silence. Mitch watched as two men hefted his eight-foot palm into the van. "What is with them and plants?" He turned away. "Come on, Jeremy. I was the neat roommate. We lived together for four years, I think you can stand a few days or however long it takes before the SEC realizes they've made a huge, tax dollar–wasting mistake."

"I think it's best if we keep our distance until this blows over."

He *did,* did he? Who the *hell* did he think he was? "Have you got a girl living with you? Is that it?"

"Yes, but no."

"Then why?"

"Because we're lucky only one of us is being targeted." Jeremy spoke in a near whisper.

"I don't feel lucky."

"I can help you better this way, buddy. If I get dragged into this investigation, too, then there's nobody on the outside."

"*I* plan to stay on the outside!"

"That's one thing I've always admired about you, Mitch. Your positive attitude."

This conversation was not making Mitch feel positive. It was making him feel slightly sick. "Why shouldn't I feel positive? You…Jeremy? Hey, man, you don't believe I've done anything, do you?" Mitch couldn't believe he actually had to ask.

Jeremy hesitated. He actually hesitated. "Let's see what the lawyer says, okay?"

"You can't make up your mind without a lawyer?" A thought occurred to him. "Do we have a lawyer yet?"

"I'm working on it."

Mitch gritted his teeth. "Work faster."

"Hey, this is a busy time. And now that you aren't here to take up the slack—"

"Slack? I'm the one who spent the entire weekend working while you were the one who went to the Cowboys game."

"With *clients.* I was with clients. I was working. You know how you hate that part of the business."

This was true, Mitch grudgingly admitted to himself. And yet, it didn't seem to be quite the same.

"Mitch, I've got to go. I want to do damage control before anyone realizes there's been damage." Mitch heard him tapping his computer keyboard. "You've got the corporate card. Check into a hotel. Try that new spa one downtown. Knock yourself out. And keep in touch." Jeremy disconnected.

Keep in touch. But from a distance.

Mitch gave his head a hard shake. Check into a spa hotel? Was Jeremy nuts?

His phone rang. He answered without looking at Caller ID. "Donner."

"Mr. Donner, this is Carson Rentals. There's a problem with your credit card. You are no longer an authorized user."

The corporate card. "I was an authorized user an hour ago when you rented me the car."

"We've received updated information—"

"Never mind." Mitch gave them Jeremy's cell number. "Tell him he can authorize the rental, or I'll drive his car. His choice."

"If you could come back to sign—"

"No. Mr. Sloane will take care of any paper work."

He clicked off and before the car rental girl could call him back, he pressed "1" on his speed dial and closed his eyes. In a situation like this, there was only one thing to do. One place to go. Two people who believed in him, which were two more than believed in him here.

"Mitch!"

At the delight in her voice, he relaxed for the first time in hours. "Hey, Mom, guess what? I'm coming home for the holidays."

Chapter Two

After Thanksgiving. At least a week. The leftovers have been eaten and those who've arrived for a "holiday visit" should have long since departed. But they haven't. They're hanging around making their parents nervous.

SHE WAS GETTING FAT. Fat, fat, fat. Wearing a retro full black slip, Kristen twisted and turned in front of the full-length mirror and vainly tried to find her hip bones, but they were hiding in the shadow made by her new stomach pooch. And if she needed more proof of fatness, Kristen had caught herself lingering on the television shopping channels when they advertised anything with elastic waists.

She couldn't even blame her mother's cooking. Oh, sure, her mother, Barbara, had cooked a turkey with trimmings for Thanksgiving. Okay, technically, she'd heated up a takeout bird along with the prepackaged side dishes, but the mashed potatoes had been made from scratch with Kristen's very own two hands.

Ah, mashed potatoes. How long had it been since

she'd scarfed down their fluffy, buttery goodness? Well, breakfast, actually. Kristen pulled on her new black skirt and tried to work up some guilt. And failed.

Had no one noticed that while the other turkey dinner leftovers had disappeared at a proportional rate, the mashed potatoes had magically reappeared meal after meal?

Kristen closed her eyes and remembered the cheese and jalapeños she'd added to yesterday's mashed-potato lunch, after which she'd drunk water all afternoon. It had been worth it. How could she have survived all that time in carbless Los Angeles without cheese and jalapeños?

And potatoes. Wonderful, glorious potatoes. They oozed warm comfort. Filled the belly. Relaxed the mind. Nature's perfect food.

There was a time when her mother wouldn't have let her eat three meals of mashed potatoes a day, but meals had been very casual since Kristen had come home. What had happened to the family dinners when they all gathered around the table and Kristen and her little sister Nicole would report on their days?

Okay, so Nicole was married now and Kristen was technically living in Los Angeles until… Oh. It was after December first, so she was technically living in her old room at her parents' house. An old room she'd expected to see in the same condition she'd left it after coming back for Nicole's wedding. Then it had been cleaned up some, but still had her furniture and curtains and her stuffed animals and trophies. It wasn't a shrine, but it was an awfully familiar-looking guest room.

However, that was all gone. No more lilac-and-white eyelet. Now the room was painted a soft sage green and held exercise equipment with a pullout sofa bed and a computer.

Because they were always working late, her parents weren't around a whole lot in the evenings. No sitting in front of the TV eating Healthy Carbolyte frozen meals for them. And no apron-clad mother slaving over a hot microwave for Kristen. Dinner—and breakfast and lunch—was grab and eat, except for Friday nights, when she and her parents linked up over takeout food.

It wasn't what Kristen had expected. But then again, the turn her life had taken wasn't what she expected. In addition to being fat, she was bored and broke, so she'd officially gone to work for her father.

It sounded worse than it was.

She slipped the matching black suit jacket off the hanger and shrugged into it. Adjusting the mighty shoulder pads so they were actually on top of her shoulders and not horrible deformities on her back, Kristen buttoned the jacket.

Not so bad. She wasn't really *fat* fat. She had put on weight, but it had smoothed the sharpness of her collarbones. Part of the extra weight had landed in her hips, of course, but some had lingered in her chest and for the first time since her Miss Sweetest days, Kristen had a hint—actually more like a strong suggestion—of cleavage.

Yes, she could actually be a salsa sushi girl without the tape.

In actuality, she was something just as bizarre. Incredibly, her father had retired doing whatever he'd done for an oil company, and had opened a private investigation agency inspired by old film noir movies, the very ones Kristen had imagined her parents watching all the time. If that wasn't a midlife crisis, then she didn't know what was. She had to give him points for being more original than going the red-convertible route. Anyway, Kristen had accepted the role of femme fatale receptionist while the freelance investigator her dad used part-time worked on a case out of state.

As it happens, someone's midlife crisis was someone else's clever marketing ploy and the place was doing a lot of business.

"Don't think about it," she whispered on an exhale and stepped into suede round-toed pumps.

Okay. Good to go. She had seamed stockings, a replica vintage black suit, a hat with a tiny veil and bright red lips. The lipstick got on everything from her fingers to her teeth to the telephone, but that gave her a real reason to whip out that silver compact and check her face.

This was actually kind of fun. Certainly better than sitting around wondering what had happened to her parents.

"Kristen?" Her mother knocked twice on her door. "Are you ready to go?"

Her mother had to give her a ride to work every day since Kristen had no car and she was supposed to open up the agency by seven-thirty. That was seven-thirty *a.m.*, so help her.

"Let me put on my gloves." The gloves had been an inspired addition to her work costume. For some reason, the hat and gloves kept her effortlessly in character.

"You look fabulous," her mother said. "Your waist

looks so tiny. I don't know why we don't go back to that look."

"You did. It was called the eighties." Kristen picked up her purse and looked her mother up and down. "You look pretty wow yourself." In an incredible alternate-universe kind of way.

Kristen simply couldn't accept that the chic woman with the streaked blond bob and professional make up was her mother. Her mother also wore a black suit. Kristen squinted. "Is that Prada?"

"Yes, but last season."

Her jumper-wearing, aproned mother not only knew what Prada was, but also worried about last-year's style?

Kristen couldn't get used to this version of her parents. That and the shoes. "Manolos?"

"Jimmy Choo."

Of course they were. "The real estate business must be good." Kristen followed her mother down the stairs.

"If you have talent and work hard." Barbara stopped abruptly at the bottom of the stairs. "I didn't mean to imply—"

"I know you didn't."

Kristen and her mother hadn't had an official heart-to-heart about Kristen's experiences in Hollywood, but then again, did they need to? It wasn't as though Kristen had been able to call home to rave about more than those stupid orange juice commercials.

Actually, they hadn't been that stupid. The residuals had supported her for many months. Had given her hope. It might have been better for her if she hadn't had that quick, but minor, success.

Anyway, this job with her surprising father could be

considered acting. Kristen felt her skirt swish against her seamed stockings. Definitely acting.

Her mother locked the door and pressed the button to open the garage. "I need to stop at Patsy Donner's and give her a check for the agency's parade sponsorship before I drop you off."

"Does Sugar Land still do that Christmas light parade?"

"Oh, my heavens, yes." Her mother blipped the car. "It's huge now. A real tourist draw, thanks to Patsy. She's worked her tail off. Sugar Land ought to put her on the city payroll. You've met her—her daughter, Kiki, was a bridesmaid in Nicole's wedding."

"Hmm." Kristen was only half listening as she got into her mother's new car. It was huge and plush for ferrying around clients to potential real estate properties.

"Mitch is living at home now, too," Barbara added.

"Who?"

"Kiki's older brother. He was a couple of years ahead of you in school. Do you remember him?"

Kristen tried to summon up a face to go with the name. She remembered a Mitch from the debate team. "Uh...kinda geeky?"

Her mother checked the rearview and backed the car out of their driveway. "Maybe in school. Not the Mitch I saw at the wedding."

Kristen shrugged elaborately. "He must not be my type or I would have remembered him." Kristen was already getting into character and liked the ennui in her voice.

"Kristen, be nice if we see him at Patsy's."

"Mom!" So much for staying in character. "I don't have to get out of the car, do I?"

"Kristen…" Barbara trailed off with a sigh.

Kristen's interfering-parent antenna prickled. "Oh, Mom, please. You aren't trying to fix me up with him, are you?"

"I merely thought—"

"No. No thinking. Besides, what kind of loser guy lives with his parents at his age, anyway?"

They'd come to a stoplight and Barbara gave one of those mother looks to Kristen. "He's here for an extended holiday visit—rather like you."

Ouch. "Guess we have more in common than I thought."

"MITCH?"

"Hang on. I'm about to beat the level forty-seven boss and then I can get the invisibility cloak."

Mitch's parents looked into his childhood room, now a cave lit only by the greenish hue of the computer monitor. He'd not only drawn the curtains, he'd put something over the windows to completely block all light. It smelled of stale Cheetos and burnt dust.

"Have you been up all night?" Patsy Donner asked, knowing that he had.

At first she didn't think Mitch would answer.

"What time is it?" he asked, eyes still on the monitor.

"Nine o'clock."

"In the morning?"

Patsy sighed. "Yes."

"Guess so."

She exchanged a look with Mitch's father. "We

wanted you to know we're going to be gone most of the day. We're working on the Christmas Light Parade."

"Mmm."

"Come with us," his father suggested. "The committee could use the help and you used to be pretty handy with Christmas lights."

"I'm good."

Robert and Patsy exchanged another look and Patsy signaled that they should confer downstairs. Clearly, something was wrong and she and Mitch's dad were negotiating the fine line between interfering in their adult son's life and parenting a child in need.

"Hey, Mom?" Mitch continued typing and stabbing the space bar.

Maybe he'd leave his den after all. "What?"

"Where did you put the laundry?"

Patsy gritted her teeth. At least he was interested in clean clothes. That could only be an improvement. "I put mine away."

"Where're my clothes?"

"Wherever you left them."

Mitch turned his head and blinked at her. "Oh." An explosion sounded and Mitch immediately began typing, showing more animation than Patsy had seen in three days. "No! Not there! Auuugh." He pushed himself away from the keyboard and stretched his arms over his head as ominous music played. "I spent four hours getting that far and now—!"

"Mitch!" She didn't want hear any computer game details. She'd heard enough about computer game conquests and battles and points and kills and levels and raids when he was eighteen. “If you want food, there’s meat and cheese for sandwiches. We’re leaving.”

She and Mitch’s dad were silent all the way down the stairs.

“Robert,” Patsy began.

“I know.” His lips compressed in a grim line.

“What do you know?”

“I know that the end of the year and tax season are his busiest times. I know that now is not the time to take a vacation. I know that he doesn’t appear to be leaving anytime soon. I know that he’s taken over my office. I know that he’s acting like he’s eighteen again.”

“But do you know why?” Patsy asked.

“No.”

“He hasn’t said anything to me, either, and I’m afraid to ask him.”

“Oh, I hear that.”

They were silent for a moment. “Well, clearly something is wrong. I don’t want to interfere in his life because after all, he is an adult—”

“Supposedly.”

“Robert,” she said reprovingly.

“There should be a book telling us what to do. *Handling Your Adult Children.* Did you notice that the how-to books just stopped after the *Getting Your Child into the College of His Choice* ones?”

Patsy laughed, then sobered. “Listen, you know Jeremy’s parents have offered to host the parade kickoff party this year?”

“And you didn’t like it because you thought it would be one huge advertising ploy for Sloane Property Development and Construction.”

"Yes, but nobody else has offered to underwrite it. So, why don't we take the Sloanes up on their offer? Then when you meet with them—"

"Me?" Robert gave her a long-suffering look.

"Yes. If I go, it'll look like I'm worried, which I am. But if you talk to Jeremy's father, it'll just be two men discussing their sons who are in business together."

"I'm not good at this," he cautioned, as he always did.

"You'll be fine," she reassured him, as she always did.

"You're going to ask me for details and I won't remember the right details."

"Just find out if they've had a fight or their business has gone bankrupt or something." She opened the hall closet. "I have to know."

"Why don't we just ask Mitch what's going on?"

"We can't do that! He'll think we're prying."

Robert gave her a puzzled look. "Aren't we?"

"Yes, but we don't want him to know!"

"But it's okay for Jeremy's parents to know?"

"No! Be subtle."

"I foresee doom." Robert took his jacket out of the hall closet. "Come with me."

He really was a sweetie. "I can't. I've got to go by Barbara Zaleski's office for that check. I'm hoping it's a biggie."

"I thought she was bringing it here at the crack of dawn."

"She was, but one of their couriers lost some real estate papers and she had to deal with it immediately. Very bad news."

"She could leave the check in our mail box."

Patsy hoped he wouldn't notice that. "I wanted to

talk to her. Her daughter, Kristen, is here visiting. You remember she was Miss Sweetest? Well, she and Mitch went to high school together. He was a couple of grades ahead of her, but—"

"Oh, no." Robert held up his hands. "No. *That's* interfering. I'll go see if the Sloanes mention anything about Mitch and Jeremy, but count me out of matchmaking."

Compromise. Ya gotta love it, Patsy thought.

He kissed her on the cheek, turned, then came back and kissed her full on the mouth.

"Mmm." She leaned against him. "What's that for?"

He smiled down at her. "To distract you."

When he smiled that way... "I'll need more distracting later."

"Absolutely." He kissed her again and left.

MITCH REALLY, *REALLY* WISHED he hadn't heard the last part of his parents' conversation. He stood at the top of the stairs, arms filled with laundry well past its prime, and waited until his mother closed and locked the front door. Then he tossed all the clothes to the bottom of the stairs and went to collect the rest.

There were a lot of T-shirts. He'd bought some guy's rock concert collection off eBay a couple of weeks ago and had been wearing them right out of the FedEx box. He hadn't really paid attention to what had happened to the ones he'd worn, but now he could see that exactly nothing had happened to them. They were precisely where he'd dropped them.

What was his mother thinking? Not about the laundry, but about Kristen Zaleski. Yeah, Mitch remembered Kristen. Perky. Popular. Pretty. And, from what he'd seen at that wedding his parents had strong-armed him into attending, pretentious.

If he weren't careful, his mother would strong-arm him into calling Kristen.

Mitch sat on his computer chair—his father's computer chair, to be accurate, since the SEC had impounded his—and collected the semicircle of T-shirts surrounding it.

His parents were probably wondering what was going on. Hell, Mitch was wondering what was going on. He couldn't believe he'd been here nearly three weeks. He hadn't heard from Jeremy, other than an acknowledgement of the e-mail Mitch sent him telling him he was at his parent's.

Maybe their e-mails were being monitored and Jeremy was being cautious. And anyone who watched television knew prosecutors went after phone records.

Jeremy had said he was handling the situation and if anybody could, Jeremy could. With his people skills, Jeremy would be far better than Mitch at clearing this mess up. But the waiting was hard. For pity's sake, when were the SEC and the FBI and who knows who else going to figure out they'd made a mistake?

On the other hand, Mitch hadn't had a vacation in a long time. A marathon gaming session was just what he'd needed. He'd enjoyed himself and he knew his parents loved having him home.

He turned to the monitor, the pile of T-shirts in his lap, and read the text messages scrolling at the bottom as he watched the action of the players from his raiding group who still survived the evil wizard who'd zapped Mitch.

Absently, he took an open bag of bite-sized chips

from next to the monitor and poured them directly into his mouth. Greasy fingers and precise keyboarding did not mix. Brushing his hands together, he started to type a reply to someone and then deleted it.

Kristen Zaleski. If his mother asked him to, Mitch had no good excuse to refuse to call her. Oh, and if he did, he'd have to borrow money from his father for the date. That could *not* happen.

Mitch ate more chips. Crunching soothed him. He needed his bank account unfrozen. Maybe it was. Temporarily abandoning the computer game, he logged onto his account, saw the red lettering and didn't bother to read the depressing notice he'd already memorized.

Before he could talk himself out of it, he phoned Jeremy.

"Hey, buddy, what's up?"

How could Jeremy sound so cheerful? "That's why I'm calling—to find out what's up."

"It's been crrrraaaazy. You know the EOY frenzy."

Did Jeremy have someone in his office? "I'm not checking on the end-of-year financial maneuverings. I'm checking on the investigation. What's the status?"

Jeremy inhaled. "No change."

"But…" How could there be no change? "What are they looking for? What looked funny to them? I can show them what I was doing. Let's speed this thing along. What's the lawyer say?"

"Didn't you get an attorney?" Jeremy's voice had lost all his frat boy affability.

Mitch's stomach felt unsettled and it wasn't because

of the chips. He reran the last conversations he'd had with Jeremy. "You said you'd take care of that."

"Oh, that's right. Conflict of interest on this end."

"You could have told me."

"Sorry." Jeremy exhaled heavily. "I guess I thought we'd know more by now. You should talk to somebody down there anyway. I'm coming to Sugar Land for Christmas—my folks are heavy into that parade thing—and we can all take a meeting then."

"My assets are frozen," Mitch reminded him pointedly. "Who am I supposed to hire—a snowman?"

"Ahhhhhh…lemme see what I can do. Hang in there. Got another call." And he was gone.

Mitch replaced the phone in its charger. So no attorney was on board? Conflict of interest? Whose interest? And "lemme see what I can do" was not, "I'm hiring one today."

Mitch knew what had happened. Jeremy had no doubt called Peter DeAngelo, the lawyer they had on retainer, and he'd probably mentioned the "conflict of interest" thing. The two of them probably thought the whole situation would be resolved quickly and Jeremy had got caught up in the end-of-year craziness and had…forgot. For something this big, Mitch should have probably hired his own attorney, anyway.

The thing was, Jeremy always came through. He drove Mitch crazy by waiting until the last minute and then would have a perfectly smooth solution to the thorniest of problems. If Mitch interfered, he always messed something up. It was always best to let Jeremy do whatever Jeremy did and not try to figure out how he did it. However, Jeremy was not the detail person Mitch was, and he was up in Dallas functioning unchecked. Who knew what kinks Mitch would have to straighten out when he returned? Whenever that would be.

He needed money. And when a Sugar Land kid—no matter how old—needed money, he went to work for The Electric Santa.

Mitch smiled at the memory of his college vacation job. During the holidays, Sugar Land overdid it on the light displays. Lining the sidewalks and yards with lights was even required in certain neighborhoods. That part was probably mostly done, but the Christmas Light Parade with the animated floats and the Town Center display would require people working right up until the last minute.

Sparky Monaghan, owner of The Electric Santa, had told Mitch that he'd always have a job with him.

Mitch decided to take him up on that.

Chapter Three

"Kristen?"

"Yeah, Dad?" She pushed her chair back from her desk until she could see across the reception area and into the open door of his office.

Carl Zaleski caught her looking and glared. "Kristen!"

Oops. She resumed her position. "Yes, Mr. Zaleski?"

"Intercom," he insisted.

Momentarily slumping and squeezing her eyes shut, Kristen straightened, pasted a professional expression on her face, and pushed the black Bakelite lever on the wooden box that sat next to the old-fashioned dial telephone. "Yes, Mr. Zaleski?"

"Kristen, would you please call The Electric Santa and make an appointment for them to decorate the office?"

Her father's voice sounded crystal clear because the intercom box was just a facade covering the thoroughly modern speaker.

And even if it weren't the latest in technology, she could also hear her father from inside his office just a few feet away.

But here at Noir Blanc appearances were important,

the gimmick that made her father's mid-life career change successful.

"Do you want them to decorate the interior as well?" she asked.

"No. You can handle decorating the office, can't you?"

"Sure," Kristen said, even as she visualized climbing a stepladder in suede pumps and a pencil skirt. Not gonna happen. And forget taking off her shoes. Seamed stockings were expensive and she didn't want to chance running them. She'd have to come after hours in her jeans.

"Are the ornaments vintage, too?" she called.

"Kristen—try to remember to use the intercom."

She pressed the lever, which was supposed to buzz the box on her father's desk letting him know she wanted to talk.

"Yes?"

She pushed her lever. "Are the ornaments vintage, too?"

"Some are and some are copies of old German glass ornaments. Expensive, but very effective."

"Sounds good." Kristen released her lever and picked up the telephone. She hated the telephone. Instead of being an actual rotary dial telephone, it was a touch-tone pad with a dial over it. To work the phone, she had to poke her fingers through the round holes.

She'd messed up her careful Revlon Red manicure before her father explained that the little plastic stick with the ball on the end that she'd found in her pencil drawer was a phone dialer. Who knew?

"Electric Santa. Let us brighten your holidays."

Hey, nice voice. Sparky must have a new manager. Kristen wondered how he'd like *her* voice. "This is

Kristen with Noir Blanc Investigations," she purred throatily. "We'd like to have you, uh, brighten our holidays." Said the right way, anything sounded suggestive.

There was silence and Kristen nearly lost it as she imagined some college kid on the other end of the line with his mouth agog. With this job, she had to take her amusement where she could.

He recovered quickly and she heard a soft, sexy chuckle. "It would be my pleasure, I'm sure." He matched her tone before briskly reciting the Electric Santa offerings. "Our standard Up On the Housetop commercial package includes outlining your roof, windows, walkways, doorway, edging of the green areas and any parking lot. The Winter Wonderland package includes lighting your landscaping. The Electric Santa Special includes your choice of Christmas display figures."

"Hmm. As intriguing as the thought of displaying a figure is, I'll have to go with the Winter Wonderland package."

"Wonderful."

Kristen could hear the smile in his voice.

"Will you need your halls decked as well?" he asked.

"No, I'll rock around my own Christmas tree."

He laughed. "I've got Noir Blanc down for one Winter Wonderland exterior."

Hmm, yes. She did like the sound of him. "So when's Santa Claus comin' to town? I wanna know when to hang up my stocking."

"Well," he drawled. "It depends on whether you're going to be naughty or nice."

Kristen grinned and then had to use her fingers to mush her lips back in place so she could keep her husky voice. "The sooner you get here, the sooner I can jingle your bells."

That prompted a nice, sexy chuckle. "Santa is harnessing his reindeer as we speak."

"Hey, Santa?"

"Yes?"

"Ditch the elves."

AFTER MITCH HUNG UP the phone, he stared at it. Holey shomoley had things ever changed in Sugar Land. It's a good thing he'd never had a call like that years ago. A teenaged guy would do something stupid like lock up the office and head toward Noir Blanc right in the middle of a business day.

Now that he was an adult, Mitch would remember to set the answering machine first.

Sparky Monaghan had told him to take calls until his schedule was full, but as far as Mitch was concerned, the lady at Noir Blanc could have all the time she wanted.

Grabbing a hooded sweatshirt—bright red with a Santa Claus face on it and The Electric Santa emblazoned across the back—Mitch headed toward the parking lot where his sleigh awaited.

And here he abandoned any pretense, all hope of cool.

He thought of The Voice on the phone. And in his mind he capitalized it. A voice like that was always capitalized. A voice like that would not, under any circumstances, be attracted to a man who drove a bright red pickup truck with a wreath on the grill and a three-foot-tall plastic Santa Claus strapped to the roof. At least it wasn't nighttime when the lights on the Santa figure flashed. A hearty "Ho, Ho, Ho!" sounded when he honked the horn, but no one needed to know that because he was not ever going to honk the horn. Not. Ever.

No, Mitch wasn't going to be cool when he met The Voice. At the best of times, accountants got a bad rap. Accountants who owned their own businesses fared better. Accountants who were living with their parents while being investigated for...for *something* had no business even mourning the loss of cool.

So Mitch had no illusions that The Voice would be wildly attracted to him. He was just curious to see her.

And, okay, he was wildly attracted to her. He didn't even know what she looked like but imagined all sorts of sultry possibilities.

She'd be a brunette, for one thing. Brunettes had depth. Brunettes had dark secrets and a sensual confidence. Brunettes toyed with lesser mortals and boy howdy, was he a lesser mortal.

On the other hand, lesser mortals were frequently underestimated. He'd go with that.

Mitch made it to Noir Blanc investigations in eleven minutes, incredibly without any incidents requiring use of the ho ho ho horn.

Noir Blanc was a free standing building in a new shopping village, a cluster of house-like structures that were home to a children's clothing boutique, a gift store, an antiques store, legal offices and an interior decorator.

Cute. After he finished with Noir Blanc, Mitch figured he'd pay a visit to them to see if The Electric

Santa had their business as well. Sparky had offered him a commission on top of his near minimum-wage salary.

Good ole Sparky. Mitch had enjoyed working for him years ago. It was amazing how he'd just fit right back in. Yeah. This was a good thing. And now he was going to meet The Voice, so working for Sparky was going to become an even better thing.

Mitch drove the Santa truck around to the side parking area. Just in case The Voice missed his arrival, he wanted that chance of coolness.

Leaping up the three steps leading to the porch, Mitch took in the old-fashioned glass door with the black-and-gold lettering and the black, white and gray paint job. Then he turned the knob and stepped into a late-night detective movie.

A ceiling fan turned lazily. Clunky wooden and leather furniture decorated the room. A coat tree was by the door and framed black-and-white film stills hung on the walls.

And there, sitting behind the reception desk, filing her nails and giving him a haughty look, had to be The Voice.

"May I help you?" she asked. Yes, The Voice. The kind of voice that greased a man's gears and seeped into all the little cracks and crevices of his brain, ready to whisper commands for him to do its bidding.

She raised an eyebrow, prompting him. Great eyebrows. Very expressive and defined. She'd spent time on those eyebrows.

"Yes," he said. He needed help. No, wait. "I mean, I'm from The Electric Santa." He tried to make that sound like something more than it was.

Her gaze flicked over him. Over his red hoodie. Lingered at the Santa Claus face on the chest.

She was not fooled that it was something more than it was.

"That was quick." She gave him a slow smile. "Are you always a fast performer?"

Mitch swallowed, conscious of his blood pounding through him in a way it hadn't pounded in a very long time. His eyes were hot. He should blink. "I do a thorough job," he managed. "No complaints."

"Ah, but do you have any repeat business?"

He stared at her mouth. Her red lips fascinated him. This was the lipstick that smeared on men's collars and got them into trouble with their wives. Heck, it would get men into trouble even if it weren't on their collars.

"Repeat business?" He managed a smile. "Once you've had The Electric Santa you're spoiled for anyone else."

She carefully set down her nail file. "Is that a fact?"

"That's," he said fervently, "a promise."

Their gazes met and held. Mitch thought there was some significant something passing between them. Significant in a good way, he hoped.

The Voice stood. Actually, it was more of an unfolding undulation. Anyway, she got to her feet and walked around the desk. And then she did something he'd never seen a woman do before, at least outside of old movies. She looked down over her shoulder as she bent her knee, and then adjusted her stocking until the black line down the back was straight.

It was, without a doubt, the sexiest thing Mitch had ever seen and not just because he could look down her blouse. This was a Woman with a capital *W*. Since her voice was already capitalized, that meant she was really something.

She lowered her leg and smiled knowingly at him. "Shall we go outside and discuss the lighting?"

"Okay." He would have said okay to anything.

This woman was not the usual Sugar Land woman. This was the woman one encountered in smoky bars in slightly seedy areas of town—some other town. She was the kind of woman with long legs, tight skirts and blouses with too many buttons undone. The kind of woman mothers warned their sons about.

The kind of woman who wouldn't even know he was alive.

"Just a moment." She leaned over her desk and pressed a black lever and Mitch's fingers curled into fists at the sight of what a tight black wool skirt could do for a woman.

"Yes, Kristen?"

"Mr. Zaleski, the guy from The Electric Santa is here and we're going to discuss the decorations."

"Fine."

She straightened and gestured toward the door.

Wait a minute. "Zaleski?" Mitch asked. "Kristen Zaleski?" It couldn't be.

She cast an uncurious, heavy-lidded look back at him as they walked across the porch. "Yes?"

The look hit him so hard in the solar plexus that he nearly missed the "yes."

This was Kristen Zaleski? This…this *woman* was the formerly perky Kristen Zaleski? And then of all things to say, he said, "So that was your father? Then why did you call him Mr. Zaleski?"

"It's more professional."

"Right."

She raised one of those remarkable eyebrows. "Have we met?"

He cleared his throat. "Actually, we have."

She negotiated the steps and turned to face him as he lumbered after her.

"Debate team? High school?" he prompted.

"Ah." She nodded, but Mitch didn't think she remembered.

"My sister was in your sister's wedding?"

That did it. "Mitch Donner?" She'd dropped the capitals from her voice.

She remembered his name! She remembered his name! But from the way she stared at him, he didn't think it was in a good way.

Well, how could it possibly be in a good way?

What she saw with those long-lashed eyes was a grown man with a kid's job. There was nothing to indicate that up until a few weeks ago, he'd owned half of a successful financial services company. Technically, he still owned half.

Technically, he was wearing a red hoodie with a Santa Claus face on it.

"Mitch Donner," she said again. "So…Mom mentioned you."

They'd been talking about him? Clearly, the situation was completely unsalvageable.

"What are you doing here?" She waved an arm

around indicating either the front of the building or Sugar Land proper.

"I'm getting ready to take measurements and give you the Winter Wonderland estimate."

"No. I mean—" she shrugged "—what are you *doing*." And this time she indicated The Electric Santa logo.

"Call it helping out an old friend."

"What do you do when you're not helping out old friends?"

Dangerous territory. "Did you know Jeremy Sloane in high school?"

"I knew *of* him and his parents still live here."

"He and I went into business together. Sloane and Donner Financial Services up in Dallas."

"Oh."

Couldn't she have looked even a tiny bit impressed?

Couldn't she stop staring at the Santa Claus face on his sweatshirt?

Okay, so she was no doubt wondering how successful his company could be if he had to take on a Christmas job. Yeah. There was that. Best not to go there. "What about you?" he asked. "I remember from the wedding that you were on your way to becoming Sugar Land's next star."

"Well, I've—I've done a few things, but it takes a while to establish yourself. I was lucky enough to be accepted into the Sofia Perlman acting studio." She said this as though he should recognize the name. "My agent called in a favor."

"Wow. So you're doing great." And he was not. At least not now. "Um…is there anything you've done that I might have seen?"

She gave him a brilliant smile. "Do you drink orange juice?"

What? "Sure."

"Well, I've done a couple of national commercials for Citrus City Orange juice."

Mitch waited for more and then realized that there was no more. "That's…that's great!" He sounded fake even to himself. "I remember that you were a persuasive speaker in debate, so you should be great at selling." *Mitch, Mitch, Mitch. You aren't doing so good.* Not to mention that he'd used the word "great," like, ninety-five times.

Her gaze flicked to the Santa logo. "I remember that you were the smart one."

Always what a guy wanted to hear from a hot babe. "It probably seemed that way because I was ahead of you in school."

"No, I'm pretty sure I remember you getting the senior debate scholarship, right?"

"That was a long time ago." And not the sort of thing he trotted out to impress women.

"Obviously, they gave it to the right guy. I mean, look at you." She gestured before crossing her arms over her chest. "You're a big success. You own your own business and it's doing so well you can afford to take all this time off."

Mitch didn't remember telling her he was taking time off. "What do you mean 'all' this time off?"

She shrugged and looked away. "Mom mentioned something about you being here on an extended vacation."

"Who said anything about extended?" His mother,

probably. "I'm here for the holidays. It's what people do. You've been here longer than I have."

"How do you know that?" She sounded as defensive as he had.

"My mother may have said something."

"I haven't been back since my sister's wedding! Pardon me for spending time with my family."

"Same here. What's the big deal? Our parents are thrilled to have us back. I can't believe people are making an issue of it."

"*Are* people making an issue of it? What have you heard?"

"Well…"

"Tell me."

He had to be honest. "Your name came up a couple of times over the weekend when I saw people who recognized me. You know, when I was lighting their houses."

"Oh, great." She looked away. "So everybody's talking about me."

"I said a *couple*. That's not everybody."

"Then it's only a matter of time." She leaned against the porch column. "Kristen Zaleski, Sugar Land's biggest flop."

A light seemed to go out inside her. Mitch didn't see the femme fatale, or the perky cheerleader, or the surprisingly good debater, he saw another person socked in the chin by life.

"You think *you're* a flop? Listen to this. The week before Thanksgiving, I arrived at the office—after spending all weekend working—to find the FBI and the SEC impounding all my files, my office furniture and even my plant." That got her attention. "Then, they take my car. Then, they do the same thing to my town house, including the plants. And then they freeze my bank accounts. So here I am, broke and living with my parents. I do have this cool job, though. Think you can top that?"

She didn't hesitate. "I changed my name to Kristie Kringle and after six and a half years of auditions, two orange juice commercials and a lot of perfume demo gigs, my agent sent me on an audition for a burlesque house. And that's when my film career aspirations ended. I sold my car for scrap and bought a one-way bus ticket home. So I, too, am broke and carless, but with a cool job."

They regarded each other solemnly. Mitch didn't know who cracked the first smile, but in moments they were grinning at each other. Mitch thought he'd never been as attracted to a woman as he was to Kristen at this moment. "I'm glad we had this chat," he said.

Kristen exhaled. "Me, too. It's such a relief to be able to relax around someone. Have you told your parents?"

"No, but they're bound to figure it out soon. They know Jeremy's parents. How about you?"

"Mine can probably figure out everything but the burlesque house."

"So we're pretty much in the same boat."

"You could say that. However, I don't believe I did anything illegal."

"I didn't either!" Mitch protested.

"That's what they all say."

"I didn't!" Mitch spoke more sharply than he intended.

Kristen didn't even blink. "So what do they think you did?"

"I don't know."

"How can you not know?"

"They wouldn't say."

"They *have* to say. Isn't that a law or something?"

One would think. "Jeremy's handling it."

Mitch looked away, which reminded him that he should be measuring. He got out his nifty laser thingamabob—they hadn't had those when he'd worked for The Electric Santa before—and pointed it to the corner of the property line.

"And Jeremy thinks...?"

She was just not going to let this go. "He doesn't know either." Mitch recorded the reading and set the parameters for the next measurement.

"Mitch?"

He ignored her, hoping she'd drop the subject. He hadn't told the entire story to anyone. He'd avoided thinking about it. But hearing it all at once like that sounded really bad. Really bad.

She touched his arm and then poked it until he looked down at her.

"What?"

"What does your lawyer say?"

He didn't answer.

"Oh. My. God. You don't have a lawyer?"

Her voice had gone kind of squeaky at the last. He missed the sultry, sexy come-hither voice she'd used earlier.

"You don't have a lawyer," she answered her own question.

"I thought it might make me look guilty if I ran out and hired a lawyer. Besides Jeremy is handling everything." Mitch strode toward the other edge of the property line. "He excels at handling."

She followed. "Is Jeremy a lawyer?"

"No. Why are you hung up on this?" He didn't want to think about it. Thinking about it made him feel slightly sick. He pointed the laser at the corner of the building.

"Because even though I've only been working for my dad a couple of weeks, it's long enough to realize that smart lawyers can get people off anything."

"Again, this is a misunderstanding." He recorded his measurement without checking to see what it was. He hoped it was right. "True, it's taking longer than I figured for them to realize they've made a mistake, but—"

"But nothing!"

Mitch walked to the edge of the building. "You want the roofline outlined, right?"

"Mitch."

"Yeah, we'll outline the roof."

"Mitch."

He looked down at her. "You're very nosy."

"I consider myself a student of human behavior and I tell you this with all sincerity: people are weird. And sneaky. And money hungry. But you, I can't figure out. Why aren't you doing something?"

Mitch measured the roof line. It was satisfying to point the tiny beam of light at things. He could pretend he was shooting them. "I thought Jeremy was working with our corporate attorney, okay? I just found out he wasn't. Something about conflict of interest. We both thought this problem with the SEC would—"

"You mentioned the FBI was also involved," she reminded him sternly.

"Well, yes, but that's because of regulations. The point is we figured this would blow over in a couple of days and I guess Jeremy…things get really busy this time of year and he…must have forgotten about the lawyer. But he works better under the gun."

He didn't like the look she was giving him. No doubt it was exactly the same look he'd give someone who told him this kind of a story. "What's it to you, anyway?" he snapped, because she was right.

"Take off your shirt."

"What?"

"The sweatshirt." She waved her hand at it. "Take it off."

Talk about a change of pace. Now here was the thing. When a gorgeous woman demanded that Mitch undress, he generally did as he was told. So it was kind of automatic that he'd drop his laser doohickey, grasp the hem of the hoodie and haul it over his head.

Kristen's gaze wandered over him. "Ah," was all she said. But she nodded when she said it. "You can put your shirt back on now."

Not the response for which he'd been hoping, but realistically, they were standing outside next to one of the main streets in Sugar Land. And it was breezy wearing just the knit shirt. So he put his sweatshirt back on. "What was that all about?" he asked as the sweatshirt popped back over his head.

"I was checking your bod."

Hello?

She went on. "You seem like a nice, decent guy and

I thought we might hang out together while we're both redirecting our lives, so to speak."

This was so far beyond what he'd dared to hope…

"I don't meet too many nice, decent guys either in acting or in the investigation business. Now call me shallow, but I like guys I'm with to have a nice body. Yours isn't bad. Some people might even say it's hot—but it's not hot enough to make up for the fact that you *apparently do not have a brain in your head!*"

Mitch picked up his laser measure. "I think I've been complimented and insulted at the same time."

"Don't strain the one brain cell you've got trying to figure it out." She crossed her arms over her chest. "Get a lawyer."

"I will."

"I mean it! I'll give you some names."

"Wait until I get paid at the end of the week."

Kristen stood in the center of the sidewalk and looked skyward. "Have you priced lawyers lately? The kind of lawyer you need gets as much per hour as you'll make in a week."

"I know that. I need the paycheck so I can afford to take you out to dinner while you're giving me the names."

She gave him a look. "You're very sure of yourself."

"I intrigue you." He recorded the last of his measurements and headed toward the truck.

She followed. "Oh, really!"

He smiled to himself. "Yes. Because you think I'm worse off than you are."

"Trust me. You are."

"And that makes you feel superior."

"If you think that, then why do you want to be around me?"

Mitch opened the door of the truck and retrieved his laptop. "Because you intrigue me."

Chapter Four

"Thanks so much for your contribution." Patsy Donner took the envelope Barbara Zaleski handed her.

Barbara waved her words away. "Thank *you* for coming by. It's been crazy this morning. I hated to ask you to make the trip over because I know how busy you are with the parade. I really admire you for taking it on."

Patsy smiled. "It's fun and really gets me in the Christmas spirit."

"You mean—alcoholic spirit?"

"Well, that, too!"

They both laughed.

"Seriously," Patsy continued, "Robert and I are at a place in our lives where we can give back. Sugar Land is our hobby. We want to retire here and anything we do now will make Sugar Land just that much better for us."

"And I can tell you that the parade and all the rest you do in the community has certainly increased the property values. People come for the parade and they like what they see of the city." Barbara's smile widened. "And being in the real estate business, I have no argument with that!"

Patsy lingered. She knew Barbara was busy. *She* was busy, but she and Barbara had something in common, something Patsy wanted to discuss. "I hear Kristen is home for the holidays."

"As is your Mitch."

"Yes."

A look passed between them. "Is it as awful for you as it is for me?" Barbara burst out.

Patsy exhaled in relief. "Possibly worse. It's as though he never left. He just..." She waved inarticulately. "It's not as though I'm not happy to see him, but he expects me to..."

"Cook? Do his laundry? Cater to him?"

Patsy closed her eyes. Someone else was going through it, too. Someone else understood. "I don't think it's dawned on him that we're actual people and not just his parents."

"Exactly." Barbara leaned against her desk. "Look at me. Do you see Betty Crocker here?"

Patsy shook her head. "He hasn't done laundry since he's been home. Some days he doesn't get dressed. I refuse to be blackmailed into cooking for him, but if I don't, he'll drink soda and eat chips *and* he leaves the empties in his room. A room that was our home office, I might add, and now is video game central."

"Kristen is carb loading and watching the shopping channels on cable. I don't dare ask when she plans to go back to California because I don't think she has any plans at all. Frankly, with that many carbohydrates in her, she can't be thinking clearly."

"But you said Kristen is working for her father. At least she's doing something. Mitch is playing computer games. He has a business to run in Dallas. What is he doing here?" Patsy didn't really expect an answer.

"Have you asked him?"

"No! I'm afraid to find out!"

Barbara laughed and groaned at the same time. "The horrible thing is, that makes perfect sense to me. I don't know about you, but having another adult in the house, even one you've given birth to is, um, limiting."

They exchanged another look. Patsy knew what she meant. "Yes. Frustrating and limiting. I don't know how to say, 'Hey, look. We've changed.'"

"'Our lives aren't revolving around you anymore,' right?"

"Exactly."

They were silent for several moments. Patsy knew she should get on with her day and let Barbara get on with hers, but it was such a relief to find someone to talk to without feeling guilty for not wanting Mitch around all the time. He was her son, after all.

Patsy glanced up to see Barbara studying her. "Patsy," Barbara began in a voice that telegraphed her intention to ask a favor.

Patsy braced herself.

"Do you think you could persuade Mitch to ask Kristen out for a movie or dinner? Maybe both? It's just…Carl and I haven't been alone in the house for weeks."

"Reverse babysitting?"

Barbara nodded. "They go out and we stay home."

Patsy thought about Robert and the hopeful twinkle in his eye when he'd left this morning. She was pretty sure she'd had the same twinkle. She was pretty sure she was twinkling now. Or maybe it was a twitch. "I like it. And I'll admit that I've kinda nudged Mitch in Kristen's direction already."

"Nudge harder."

"Gotcha." Patsy exhaled. "Thanks again for the check and the talk."

"It was my pleasure." Barbara chuckled. "Or I hope it will be."

WELL, THAT WAS...intriguing, Kristen decided, sticking with the word of the day. She liked that look Mitch had given her just before he printed out an estimate and drove off in The Electric Santa truck. Not easy to pull off a look of self-confident interest under the circumstances.

Some people might be fooled by the dorkmobile, but Kristen, having spent years living in the land of professional fakes, knew the real thing when she saw it. And any man who could not only drive a red truck with a Santa torso on the hood, but also honk a ho ho ho horn as a goodbye, had no masculinity issues whatsoever.

"Embrace the kitsch!" Kristen called just after he'd honked.

Mitch actually seemed like a nice guy in the good-nice way and not the only-his-mother-loves-him way. He might possibly be a little on the plain vanilla side for her, but sometimes a girl's just gotta yen for smooth vanilla after a run of Rocky Road.

She watched until the truck turned the corner. Definitely time for a break from Rocky Road.

Kristen climbed the steps, pulled open the etched glass door and nearly ran into her father.

He was shrugging into a leather jacket and had left his overcoat and fedora on the brass coat tree.

"Ooo, surveillance." Kristen knew the signs.

Her father smiled gently. "Nora Beckman. She just left the house to go Christmas shopping."

"Oh." Nora was a recovering alcoholic and the holidays were difficult. Her husband, Ralph, hired them to discreetly head her off at the town liquor store. To Kristen, it was a touching, face-saving gesture. He trusted his wife, but was providing support in case she needed it. "In that case, I hope you don't find her."

"I hope I don't, either." But her father didn't look too hopeful.

Kristen thought wistfully of the kind of love Ralph Beckman had for his wife. It was rich with an understanding ripened by time, the kind of love nice, decent, emotionally mature men had for their life partners. Oddly, the same kind of men who wouldn't mind driving red trucks bearing plastic Santa torsos when the situation called for it.

Not that Kristen was having any such thoughts about Mitch for herself, because she could stand only so much vanilla before she needed to crunch on some Rocky Road.

Kristen returned to her desk and started to work on the routine background investigations her father assigned to her.

A significant portion of Noir Blanc's business came from women investigating the background of men they were dating, a practice Kristen heartily endorsed after being burned a few times herself. Besides, she discovered that she really enjoyed snooping. Yeah, she was ready to call it character research for her acting in case anyone asked, but no one did.

Noir Blanc had a few male clients, as well, but they

were a definite minority. Kristen didn't know if men were more trusting in the dating scene, but from what she'd seen, they shouldn't be. Maybe the men only hired Noir Blanc when they were already suspicious because Kristen had discovered way too many women out there giving the sisterhood a bad name.

And speaking of trust, Mitch sure trusted his partner. Yeah, friendship and loyalty and all that were admirable but Kristen didn't think Mitch's situation was anything like the realistic trust Ralph Beckman had for his wife. Maybe she was just overly cynical. However… However, it was none of her business. Literally.

She ran the routine checks and didn't find any red flags, which would guarantee a nice holiday for their clients. Everybody was on the up-and-up this season. Good will toward men and all that. After writing the reports, she printed them out and put them on her father's desk.

Finished. All done. Phones silent. Computer humming. Lipstick fresh. Nails filed. Thumbs twiddling.

And so Kristen did what she knew she'd been going to do ever since Mitch had honked the ho ho ho horn. She ran a background check on him.

KRISTEN ZALESKI'S LIPS exactly matched the red Christmas lights The Electric Santa used, so naturally, Mitch thought about her the rest of the day. Stringing lights didn't exactly require deep thought—other than remembering how many lights he'd strung together so he didn't overload the circuit—which meant Mitch had plenty of time to think. About Kristen. And her lips. And other body parts.

He tried to recall any high school memories, but the Kristen that came to mind bore no resemblance to this Kristen, and that was fine with him. He liked this Kristen better.

On the way home, Mitch stopped at a video rental store and wandered down the classics aisle. He identified the film noir movies by the actresses on the cover of the case—they looked just like Kristen, except that they were in black-and-white and Kristen, or rather her mouth, was in living color. Christmas red, to be precise.

Mitch picked a handful of videos with names like KISS ME DEADLY, DARK PASSAGE and THE BIG SLEEP, added a few packs of microwave popcorn and a two-liter bottle of Coke with lime—just in case there was a trace of vitamin C in it—and headed for home.

NOT ONLY WAS HE plain vanilla, he was white bread. Cream of wheat. Macaroni and cheese—hey. Macaroni and cheese. Yum. Kristen had never been a mac and cheese eater as a child, but the idea of warm, creamy goodness suddenly appealed.

They were running out of potatoes, anyway.

But back to Mitch. Yes, he was macaroni and cheese. No outstanding warrants. No arrests. No unpaid traffic tickets—or paid ones, either. No ominously sealed juvenile records. Paid his credit cards off every month, no glitches in the credit rating, except—what the heck was this? A big, old, fat bar, that's what it was. A big, old fat bar that turned into a wall. Even the best software programs Noir Blanc had couldn't get past it.

Wow. Mitch had mentioned something about his accounts being frozen, but this was subzero. Kristen backed up and tried to check out last month's information, but couldn't get into that, either.

So she went fishing. Back to the credit reports. This time, she studied which cards he had and which companies had requested his file.

Anderson Personnel was on top. They'd requested his file last March. Now why was a personnel company requesting Mitch's personal credit report? His company's profile, sure, but why Mitch's own data? Was Mitch job hunting back then? And why would he job hunt when he owned his own company?

Kristen searched for info on Anderson Personnel and discovered it was a holding company. Okay, what and who were they holding? Texas Rhinestone Corporation. Rhinestones needed a corporation? Maybe not, because TRC turned out to be Longhorn Entertainment's parent company. And Longhorn Entertainment owned…Kristen searched and clicked. Fruit? The Coconut Club. Big Bananas. Tutti Fruiti. Miss Melons. Cherries Jubilee.

Somehow, Kristen didn't think she was looking at fruit-of-the-month clubs. Beefsteaks. Whipped Creme. Oh, how nice. They'd branched out into other food groups.

Her stomach growled. She ignored it.

Adult clubs. Had to be. Something about rhinestones and entertainment pointed Kristen in that direction. Frankly, she had a live-and-let-live attitude toward the adult entertainment industry as long as it didn't live too close—or try to pawn off burlesque as family entertainment.

She briefly wondered if the sushi and salsa place was connected—that was food, wasn't it?—but decided it wasn't worth the effort of researching. She'd stick with the fruits.

Now, where were these places? And how were they connected with Mitch? One of his ick-factor clients?

Why did "ick factor" immediately bring to mind Jeremy Sloane? Was it because "ick" rhymed with "slick"? She only had a high-school-aged memory, but she'd bet he looked about the same—slick in a carefully styled young-businessman-at-a-prayer-breakfast-with-the-boss kind of way.

He'd been the student council vice president, a member of the mixed chorus, the football team manager—a position reserved for those who couldn't play but wanted to pretend they were a part of the action. Kristen had a sudden vivid memory of Jeremy handing out water to the players on the sidelines. She'd been on the drill team and they always lined up early behind the team to prepare for their halftime show. The players, oblivious to anything but the action on the field, had tossed the plastic squirt bottles and cups to the ground and dirty water had splashed onto some of the drill team's white boots.

Kristen remembered their lieutenant yelling at the players about it. An assistant coach—the hot one they all had a crush on—sent an annoyed look first at them, and then at Jeremy. Yeah, it had been Jeremy. She remembered his carefully parted hair. And then she remembered how he took a towel and went down the line wiping their white boots as they stood at attention.

Kristen had only been relieved to get the splashes of mud off but now she wondered how he'd felt. No big deal? Or the ultimate humiliation?

She hadn't seen his expression because they'd been trained to keep motionless and their eyes forward. And, frankly, until this moment, Kristen hadn't given the incident—or Jeremy Sloane—a second thought.

Now she did. He was on the short side in high school, if Kristen recalled correctly. With the experience of years, she figured that he must have had short-man syndrome even then. It was easy to find a current picture of him on the Internet. Lots of pictures of him, as a matter of fact.

Kristen clicked through them, noticing the ritzy locales, the parties, the women and all the props men with inadequacy issues surrounded themselves with to feel important. Oh, she so knew the type.

Or, again, she could just be overly cynical.

However, unless he was dating only six-foot-four models, he was still short. Good-looking, though, if a woman went for the carefully groomed, capped teeth, buffed nails type rather than the could-use-a-haircut-red-Santa-hoodie-wearing type.

Hypothetically.

And because it was easier to investigate Jeremy than Mitch, Kristen did so.

Within ten minutes, Kristen had figured out their working relationship. Mitch was not in a single one of the "see and be seen" pictures. Jeremy was clearly the people person and brought in their business. Mitch must be the brains. Since in Kristen's opinion, he was currently acting pretty brainless, it was a scary thought.

But if it worked for them, great. Only not so great if Mitch was being investigated and Jeremy wasn't. Jeremy could make a good case for denying any knowledge of what Mitch had been doing. Whatever that turned out to be.

Kristen reached into her file drawer and removed the bottle of water she kept out of sight. Plastic bottled water didn't fit with the decor. After taking a swig, she put it back and stared at her computer screen. Tapping her Revlon Red nails—a new habit she kinda liked—Kristen considered her next move.

She wanted access to the private stuff about Jeremy Sloane, except there were ethics involved here. She could justify investigating Mitch because of her personal involvement with him. Or potential personal involvement. But investigating his business partner was a stretch. Mitch would have to hire Noir Blanc and Kristen knew he wouldn't do that. There needed to be paperwork to document an investigative request and if they were subpoenaed—not likely—that paperwork would be examined.

Her father ran a squeaky clean operation and Kristen wasn't going to jeopardize that.

What to do, what to do.

Start that paper trail, for one thing. So she was her own client. She'd be up front about it. And she'd use one of their Dating Security packets, too. She was allowed to date, right? And…and maybe she'd like to invest, too. Maybe…maybe she became interested after meeting Mitch. And…and she was thinking of using his financial services. Yeah. That would do it. Never mind that she didn't have anything to invest. She was looking ahead. Planning for the future.

And if investigating whether Mitch was on the up-and-up—there were those nasty blocks and bars in his records, after all—she needed to delve into his company, because of her future investing and all, well, a girl couldn't be too careful these days. Therefore, didn't it make perfect sense to investigate his company and, by extension, his partner in crime? Bad choice of words.

Kristen got into character. "Why, Mr. District Attorney—" insert batting of eyelashes "—when I couldn't find out anything about Mitch, what was I to do? I mean, I could have lost my life savings as well as my virtue."

Oh, yeah. *That* would be convincing. Maybe she should go for the cynical-burned-by-life-yet-still-hopeful type. "Mr. District Attorney, I'd been burned before—" insert Scarlett O'Hara I'll-never-be-hungry-again expression "—and I wasn't going to get burned again."

Bingo. She could so sell that if she had to.

Okay. Paperwork done. Everything on the up-and-up. Commencing investigation of Sloane and Donner Financial Services.

Noir Blanc owned various software programs that provided access to detailed databases and subscribed on a per-use basis to other, more specialized services. That's where she figured she'd find all the dirt. Kristen felt mildly guilty for running up a tab, especially when she was her own client. She should just stop. It wasn't as if Mitch's problems were *her* problems.

But…but she had a hunch. Carl Zaleski was a great believer in hunches and intuition and she told herself he'd be pleased. Her father claimed that hunches, intuition and the ever popular "gut feeling" were actually the result of sharpened observation skills. He'd been trying to hone Kristen's skills by having her relieve him on boring stakeouts and following people. Honestly, it was great acting training. But she didn't feel detective-like, even though she thought she was a fairly good observer of human nature. And, though her father encouraged her—probably hoping she'd have some marketable skill to fall back on—she'd never intuited anything and the only hunch she'd felt was the ache in her shoulders from leaning on the steering wheel of their car.

Until now. Now, she was feeling something and it was kind of a kick. An expensive kick, she winced as she rang up a $29.95 charge for access to yet another financial database. The answers were out there. She just had to ask the right questions. And it seemed that the right questions were more about Jeremy than Mitch.

Time passed. Shadows fell. Kristen's father called from a liquor store fifty-two miles away. As she talked with him, Kristen stretched one arm at a time over her head and then stood to get the circulation moving in her legs. "Mrs. Beckman made you, huh Dad?"

"I'm not sure. She's still sitting in the car, poor woman. I'm hoping she'll turn around and drive back without my interference." Carl Zaleski sighed. "You might as well go on home. Close up for me?"

"Sure. Hey, I'm working on something. You know Mitch Donner?"

"I…uh…"

"Oh, come on. We know you and Mom and his parents have been talking about us."

There was silence.

"Dad?"

"I can't remember if I'm supposed to admit that or not. I'm just not good at this sort of thing!"

Kristen laughed. "Dad! You're an investigator!"

"Right. Not a matchmaker. Oh, for the love of Mike, I know I shouldn't have said that." He sighed heavily.

"It's okay. Mitch and I'll probably hang out together."

Sounding hopeful, he asked, "Is that anything like going on a date?"

"Yes, Dad."

"Could you tell your mother that I had something to do with it?"

Kristen smiled. "Actually, you did when you had me look into Christmas decorations. He's working for The Electric Santa."

"Why is he doing that?"

Kristen didn't want to tell her father the whole story just yet. "He has issues and he told me all about them. The thing is, he's not the kind of guy who should have these issues. Something isn't right."

"Kristen! You have a hunch." Her dad sounded so delighted.

"Yeah…about that. I hired myself, since I was thinking of hanging—dating Mitch." She waited.

"That sounds reasonable."

"This hunch is proving expensive," she told her father bluntly.

"It's your first one. You'll get more efficient. Go with your hunch until you find something or you're satisfied that there's nothing to find."

"That's just it—I've found a bunch of stuff, but I don't know what it all means."

"Well, you know, this business isn't as easy as

people think, just the way it isn't the glamorous job the movies make it out to be."

Kristen rolled her eyes at his patronizing father-knows-all tone.

"What are you looking into?" he asked.

"Financial sites. I keep getting 'flagged' messages and 'investigation pending, access denied' and contact so and so with any information—"

"Kristen," her father's voice changed instantly. "You are not to have anything to do with—"

"No, no, no. This doesn't have anything to do with Mitch, but with his partner and their company. But Mitch is the one the SEC and the FBI are after."

"*Kristen*!"

"Dad, give me some credit."

After a short silence, he grumbled. "You need to fine-tune your hunches. Tomorrow, I'll take a look at what you've got if you like."

"Thanks, Dad."

"You're going to drive me to drink—how convenient that I'm sitting in a liquor store parking lot."

Kristen grinned. "You're a good dad."

He snorted. "Say that again when your mother can hear."

Kristen cradled the heavy receiver and was still chuckling when the phone rang again. "Yes, I'll tell her!"

"Tell who what?" her mother's voice asked.

"Mom!"

"Is that the way you answer the office phone?"

"I was just talking to my great and wonderful dad who is currently parked at a liquor store in La Marque."

Barbara didn't miss a beat. "Nora Beckman?"

"Yep."

Her mother inhaled. "Alcoholism is such a nasty disease and this is a tough time of year. Maybe she needs a distraction. I'll give Patsy Donner a call and see if there's something Nora can do with the light parade."

Kristen shook her head. "Oh, that was smooth, Mom. Were you always this slick when I was growing up?"

"What are you talking about?"

"Working Patsy Donner into the conversation so you can ask whether I've connected with Mitch yet."

"I must be out of practice. So? You and Mitch?"

"Why do you care whether or not I go out with him?"

"Because you're spending too much time sitting on the couch," her mother answered.

"I'm working for Dad all day!"

"And sitting on the couch all night."

Kristen groaned. "Mom."

"Okay, we won't talk about Mitch or your spreading hips. So that leaves the rest of your life. What's up?"

Never mind the spreading hips, Kristen didn't want to think about her career, or her lack of one just then. She'd anticipated the question or something like it sooner or later, but she'd really hoped for later. "Point taken. And I do appreciate you holding back on the questions for so long."

"Kristen, you're an adult. We're your parents and we love you. When you're ready to talk, we'll listen."

"Thanks." Kristen had to swallow hard.

"But if you don't talk soon, it's our God-given right to bug you about it."

"I know." Time for a distraction of her own. "By the way, Mitch is a cutie. He's working for The Electric Santa and came by today. We're going out to dinner—after he gets paid."

Kristen enjoyed the ensuing silence.

"Uh..."

Kristen couldn't help teasing her mother. "Careful what you wish for!"

"Kristen..." There was a wealth of parental warning and concern in the way her mother said her name.

"It's okay, Mom." Kristen briefly brought her mother up to speed on Mitch's situation. "Maybe you can help me with some of this real estate stuff I've found. For instance, did you know that Jeremy Sloane's dad owns a construction company?"

"Oh, yes. Let's not get into this on the phone. I really called to tell you that I'm waiting to go to an after-hours closing and to see if you could catch a ride home with your father. But since he's not there—"

"Take your time. I want to keep working on this. So I'll see you when I see you, okay?"

"All right. Thanks, sweetie."

"Love you, Mom. Bye."

Kristen intended to get right back to work, but instead, she let her mind wander to her acting career, or lack of one. She'd been trying to live life without acting to see if she could. To see if anything else interested her. But she'd turned this job for her father into an acting gig and everyone she researched became fodder for characterization.

Kristen didn't know where she got this fascination for immersing herself into characters. No one else in her family had ever acted. Her childhood was fine, she was fairly popular in school, and had suffered no more than an expected amount of teenaged angst, so she wasn't trying to escape anything or anyone. Still, she thought she had a talent for bringing characters to life.

Or was she kidding herself?

Maybe. Probably. But she had a feeling she wasn't the only one.

Kristen logged into yet another real estate site and stared at a screen with a whole lot of words and not any interesting pictures of properties. These names were beginning to sound familiar which meant she was due for a break. Too bad. No breaks when she was paying for access by the minute.

Still reading, she stood up and stretched, stomped her feet and sat right back down again. She had definitely seen some of these names before. They'd been buried within the Russian nesting doll–like structure of companies that started with that personnel company that had queried about Mitch's credit report.

But was that something bad? It wasn't illegal to have holding companies. And a credit query wasn't illegal, either. And so what if some of those companies showed up more than once? And so what if Mitch's partner's name showed up, too? And so what if Mitch's partner's father's construction company showed up, as well? Maybe Jeremy's dad had thrown business their way. Nothing illegal about helping offspring. Look at Kristen.

And yet she felt she was missing something. Which meant Mitch was missing something.

Kristen added to her notes. She was using a cool fountain pen, which made the tedious work marginally better, and a yellow legal pad that turned the ink a funky greenish black. There was probably some software program for what she was doing, but Kristen was rusty on spreadsheets and now was not the time for a tutorial.

She was so engrossed in her columns and arrows and patterns that she started when the door opened and her mother walked in.

"You scared me!" A big drop of ink blotted Kristen's notes.

"I honked a couple of times." Barbara hesitated.

"Oh, don't say it."

"What? That you should have locked the door?"

"Yeah, that."

"Okay." Her mother came to stand next to her and looked at the screen. "What have you got?"

Kristen was using a tissue to soak up the ink blot. "Names and companies. I'm looking for a pattern."

"For what?"

"I don't know. It would help if I did. I mean, some of these companies are buying and selling property so fast. And what's with all the different names? One guy has thirteen. Jeremy's father has a bunch."

Her mother went still. "Really."

"Yeah—take a look while I wash the ink off my fingers." Kristen curled them into claws around the tissue and hunched as she stood. "I'm merely an ink-stained wretch," she said in a quavery voice while limping toward the bathroom. "Working for my daily crust of bread..."

When she returned—was ink always that hard to wash off?—she found her mother sitting in front of the computer. She'd turned over the page with the inkblot and was writing on the one beneath. Writing a lot, Kristen noticed.

"Turn around."

"Why?"

"I'm typing in my password."

"Oh, Mom!"

Barbara gave her a look—one Kristen had never seen before and one that had her turning around pronto.

"What are you doing? Accessing some secret, legally iffy Web site you don't want me to know about?" She tried to make it a joke, but it didn't quite come off. Well, she'd never been a comedienne.

"Yes," her mother replied.

Yes? "You're kidding. Aren't you? I was."

"No."

And that was the moment of Kristen's parental epiphany. Her parents really *had* changed. Or more likely they'd shrugged off the parent role and were acting more like the people they were when they weren't being her parents, if that made sense. Parents as people. What a concept.

"That bastard."

Whoa, now she *knew* they'd changed. "Uh, Mom?" Kristen turned around.

"I need to trade information—may I use your notes?" Barbara's voice was clipped.

"Sure," Kristen answered before thinking better of it "—except don't do anything that'll hurt Mitch."

Silence.

"Is there anything that'll hurt Mitch?" she asked in a small voice.

Barbara gave her a long look. "That depends."

"I don't like the sound of that."

"I don't like the looks of this." Her mother waved at Kristen's notes.

"You mean I actually found something?"

"You found pieces and I'm going to try to find the links. May I?"

Kristen nodded and immediately felt queasy. For heaven's sake, she hardly knew Mitch, and yet, here she was, worried on his behalf. She thought about his smile and that stupid Santa hoodie. She thought about the abs beneath the stupid Santa hoodie. Kristen had developed a theory about potential relationships based on abdominal development. Too squishy and that meant a desk job and no time for a girlfriend. Or a guy who didn't care and wouldn't put in any effort. A well-defined six pack required hours at the gym and thus meant no time for a relationship and an attitude that girls were supposed to be grateful to be noticed at all.

Mitch had girlfriend abs. Defined enough to show that he'd made an effort, definitely cared, but still had time to spare for the right relationship.

Kristen watched her mother's fingers dance over the keyboard. She would have made more money temping if she'd typed that well. "Wow. I didn't know you could type like that."

Without taking her eyes from the screen, Barbara commented, "I'm part of the generation where women were nurses, teachers or secretaries. I went for secretary. I remember what a big deal it was when our school got electric typewriters."

"Mom."

Her mother smiled to herself, but as Kristen watched the smile shrank. "Sloane Property Development and Construction. They really like their name on things, don't they?"

Kristen figured it was a rhetorical question.

Glancing at Kristen's handwritten notes, Barbara grimaced. "Why didn't you set up a spreadsheet with this information?"

"It's been awhile since computer class."

"I'm going to set one up for you." Barbara had already opened the software. "Then you can input the information while I make a couple of phone calls."

Kristen watched for a few minutes and tried to remember anything about spreadsheets. Not happening.

"Okay. You're set." Her mother pushed the chair back from the desk. "I'm going to use Carl's office phone. I don't want a record on my cell."

Kristen stared after her. "You're scaring me."

"Cell phone calls aren't secure. Remember that."

"Dad's rubbing off on you."

Her mother smiled over her shoulder. "Not often enough."

"Mother!"

Her mother laughed as she shut the office door.

Type, Kristen instructed herself. *Type and do not go there*. She stared at the closed door behind which her mother was doing who-knew-what. *Do not go anywhere*.

Chapter Five

Mitch popped in a cassette of his third black-and-white movie of the night. Since he'd left home, his parents had upgraded to a DVD player and he'd poked around until he'd found the old video machine in the guest room closet.

That room had been his sister Kiki's room and it still looked girly with the pastel walls, her old white-painted furniture and the blue-and-white Chinese-looking bedspread.

Whereas his room had become the office-slash-gym and the old furniture was long gone.

Mitch had carried the VCR into the den, connected the appropriate wires with only a couple of miscues, shoved in the first of the tapes and settled back with a bag of microwave popcorn.

He liked THE BIG SLEEP with Bogey and Bacall, because if he squinted and stared at her mouth, Lauren Bacall reminded him of Kristen. He could see the whole thing Noir Blanc had going now and wondered if Kristen liked it, or just tolerated it.

These were some kind of women, he thought during

the second movie. Tricky women. Bad news women you were drawn to, desperately wanting to rescue them so they'd be able to be with you. Women being blackmailed. Women who betrayed. Women who loved unwisely.

He enjoyed sitting in the dark, watching the light and shadows play across the faces of the actors as their characters made really poor life choices. Mitch didn't know why all this doom and gloom appealed to him, only that it did.

His parents arrived home midway through the third video.

"Mitch?" They appeared in the doorway.

"Are you alone?" his mother asked.

"Yeah, why?"

"Because of The Electric Santa truck blocking the drive way," Robert reminded him.

It was the first time he'd driven the truck home since he'd started working there. "Oh, sorry. I'll move it." Mitch paused the movie, stood and dug in his pocket for the key.

His father was staring at the red hoodie Mitch had left on the sofa and his mother had bent to pick up the empty popcorn bags. She straightened, compressing the bags. Both his parents gazed at him silently.

"Hey, I was going to pick those up."

"Really?" Patsy nudged the empty two-liter Coke bottle with her toe.

Mitch picked up the bottle. "Um, yeah. After the movie."

They glanced at the frozen image on the screen. Or maybe they were looking at the DVD player he'd set on the floor and the VCR that he'd propped precariously on the shelf above the TV, a shelf that had previously held a silver-framed wedding photo of his sister flanked by an engraved silver tray given to his father when he was salesman of the year and an engraved silver bowl presented to his mother by the City of Sugar Land. Everything was on the floor now.

"The video rental place didn't have copies of the movies I wanted on DVD."

"Okay," said his mother without expression.

Mitch could tell she was holding back.

"And the truck?" asked his father.

"Oh, yeah. I'm working for The Electric Santa again."

There was silence. Mitch figured that was probably for the best, but if he thought about this situation from his parents' point of view—and he didn't really want to—he would want an explanation. Only Mitch knew they wouldn't like the real explanation and he certainly didn't want them to worry. "These movies are a nice contrast," he said to fill the silence. "You know flashing lights, bright colors and Christmas frenzy during the day, bleak people with doomed lives in black-and-white at night."

His parents looked at each other and seemed to communicate in that mysterious parental way. "We've had a lot of Christmas frenzy today, ourselves," his mother said.

His dad reached down and shook the bag Mitch had left on the coffee table. "Got any more popcorn?"

"Yeah. I bought two three-packs."

"Lite, or with butter?" Robert asked.

"Butter."

Mitch's dad inhaled and closed his eyes. "Real butter or movie butter?"

"It said real butter on the package."

"Robert," Mitch's mother warned.

"Patsy?" he pleaded.

"I give up." She shook her head and laughed. "You two go shuffle the cars and I'll pop the popcorn. Then we'll watch the end of the movie together."

"Works for me." Could it be that Mitch had escaped an inquisition?

"Yes! Real buttered popcorn!" His father pumped a fist as they walked toward the driveway.

"Dad." Mitch grinned.

"Oh, you don't know what it's been like. No salt, no bacon, no butter, no carbs—except she's kind of over that—but no sugar and no egg yolks. I put my foot down about the herbal tea. She's gonna kill me with all this healthful eating."

Mitch still grinned, even though he was aware that his father was filling the silence to keep from questioning him. He touched his father's arm when they got to The Electric Santa truck. "Thanks." He figured his dad would understand.

Without looking at him, his dad asked, "Are you okay?"

Mitch thought of Kristen's skepticism. "I think so."

"You should know so."

"You're right." Mitch nodded. "I should."

"Need help finding out?"

Again he thought of Kristen. "I've got help."

"THANKS SO MUCH for all your help." Kristen's mother hung up the telephone and called to Kristen's father. "The code is RE6SL94PDOR and the year you're looking for."

"What if I don't know what year I'm looking for?" he bellowed from his office.

Everyone was getting a little testy, Kristen thought. Low blood sugar, no doubt.

Her parents had commandeered both computers, which left Kristen sitting in the waiting area trying not to bite her fingernails. She hadn't had an urge to bite her nails in years and now, even faced with her perfect and difficult-to-do-by-herself manicure, she felt like nibbling a red thumbnail.

Maybe she should offer to make a hamburger run.

Maybe she'd make a hamburger run and swing by Mitch's house and bring him back to the office to see how totally messed up his life was. Or was about to be. Depending.

Carl Zaleski had returned from following Nora Beckman, who had resisted temptation, bless her heart. Then he'd pretty much taken over from Kristen. With Barbara interpreting a lot of the real estate info, they'd found that essentially, Mitch's company had funneled substantial investment money from clients into companies that turned out to deal primarily with, or were owned by, Jeremy Sloane's father.

But that made it sound so much simpler than it was. Getting to that info had been tedious and difficult, as it was meant to be. Connections were tangled and obscured and it was only by luck—pure luck—that anything suspicious had been uncovered. Luck that Kristen had time to keep poking around because her parents were running late. Luck that her mother knew real estate and was able to connect the pieces and fill in the gaps. And if Barbara couldn't fill in the gaps, then she'd contacted colleagues who could.

Yes, Mitch was oh, so very lucky that he'd confided

in Kristen and she could hardly wait to tell him and show him how clever she—and her parents—had been. She'd succeeded at something for a first time in a long while and success felt good.

Kristen was still in the throes of self-congratulation when both parents gasped in unison. That couldn't be good.

Her father came out of his office to stand behind her mother and stare at the computer monitor as though he couldn't believe what he'd seen on his.

"What?" Kristen got to her feet.

Her parents just looked at her.

"*What?*" She headed toward the desk as her mother clicked off the screen.

"Barbara," Carl Zaleski murmured.

"What did you find?" Kristen demanded.

"She can't handle it." Her mother spoke without moving her lips.

"I heard that. What can't I handle? Scratch that. I can handle it. I can handle and have handled more stuff than you might guess." What could they have found? "I've handled rejection. Lots of rejection. And bad news." They weren't looking at her. "Weird stuff." That got their attention. "Yeah, really weird stuff that we don't have in Sugar Land."

"Don't be so sure," Barbara murmured, again without moving her lips.

"I can still hear you. Now come on."

"What do you think, Barb? Should we tell her Mitch owns GBE?"

"GBE? What's GBE?"

"Nice one, Carl." Barbara's lips were moving plenty

now. To Kristen she said, "GBE is Golden Boy Enterprises."

"That doesn't sound like Mitch. Besides, his hair is brown."

"She does have a unique take on a situation," her father commented.

"Maybe if I knew what the situation was, I could be less unique and more relevant."

"No, you misunderstand. I *like* your fresh eyes. You bring a new interpretation to the facts."

Barbara gave him a puzzled look. "But facts are true by definition. You don't interpret truth."

"*You* do," Carl scoffed. "Truth: a tiny poorly maintained shack becomes a charming fixer-upper. Or a handyman's special starter home. Or a prime lot with a tear down. Or a property with investment potential."

"I can't believe you've actually been listening to me all these years! Why, Carl, you sweetheart."

"Hey!" Kristen made the time-out sign with her hands. "Nice attempt at distraction, but it didn't work. What is Golden Boy Enterprises and why is it bad that Mitch owns it?"

Her mother made a face and switched the monitor back on. "GBE owns Anderson Personnel."

Something about that name seemed familiar. "A personnel company? Wait a minute." Kristen ignored the spreadsheet she'd spent the last couple of hours typing on and looked at her notes. "That's the company I started with. The one that owns companies that own companies." Her eyes widened. "That means Mitch owns those strip clubs!"

FRIDAY AND PAYDAY couldn't come soon enough, as far as Mitch was concerned. It wasn't the kind of paycheck he was used to, but as long as Kristen didn't go for vintage champagne, he had enough for dinner and whatever.

It was the "whatever" that he dwelt on. He hoped there would be a "whatever," but the scope of it would be entirely up to Kristen.

He knew she was thinking about him. He'd installed lights on the outline of the Noir Blanc building and The Electric Santa had booked the rest of the little shopping area as well, so he was on outlining duty this week. He'd fill in the rest of the decorations next week.

He might have taken a little too much time with Noir Blanc, but it was all those windows he had to outline. The angle of the partially opened blinds gave him a perfect interior view from his vantage point on the ladder.

And Kristen, well, Kristen had a habit of swiveling in her chair and watching him when she was talking on the telephone.

Mitch pretended he didn't notice at first but she'd give him these speculative up-and-down looks that weren't ignorable. That look was straight out of the old film noir movies and, having watched about a dozen of them now, he knew what happened next.

The woman of the world drew the man in to do her bidding, that's what happened next.

Mitch made several unnecessary trips up and down the ladder to mitigate the effects of that look. Honest to Pete, that woman could make his blood run hot and cold at the same time. She distracted him and when a guy was working with a staple gun and wires as he stood on a ladder, he didn't need distractions.

Kristen got up from her desk and Mitch breathed easier as he watched her walk over to the coffee pot. She'd removed her jacket and was wearing a white blouse and a skirt that molded to her body. Any tighter and she wouldn't be able to sit down. He didn't know how she was able to sit now.

The women in the movies wore those skirts, even the ones without money. They'd sit and cross their legs, just like Kristen. Mitch had never noticed the whole leg crossing thing before. And they looked classy, just like Kristen. And worldly, just like Kristen. And knowing, just like Kristen.

And he was becoming obsessed, just like the helpless men.

Mitch stopped stapling and lowered his arms to let the blood flow back into them.

He needed work. His real work. He needed to fill his mind with numbers and percentages and interest rates. That was all that was wrong with him.

There was nothing particularly obsession-worthy about Kristen. A tight black skirt and a pair of red lips. Big deal.

At that moment, the door opened and she came out onto the porch. "Hot chocolate?"

He shivered. He'd forgotten The Voice.

"You're cold. Take it."

She reached up and he automatically took the heavy white china mug even though he wasn't a fan of hot chocolate and he certainly wasn't cold.

"Thanks." He took a sip. "Good." In a powdery, too diluted, instant kind of way.

Kristen smiled and hugged her arms. Mitch, who had

considered descending the ladder and joining her on the porch stayed right where he was because, from his vantage point, her modestly unbuttoned blouse wasn't so modest.

Ignoring the undissolved cocoa lumps floating in the foam, he took a swallow and burned his tongue.

That was quick karmic payback. Now he wasn't going to feel guilty for taking in the view.

"I realize you're the professional and all, but should you really be using a staple gun with wires and electricity?" she asked.

"No." He worked a lump of cocoa mix against the roof of his mouth with his tongue. He didn't want to chew his cocoa in front of her since she'd been so thoughtful to bring it to him.

"And yet, you are stapling. Are you always such a rule-breaker?"

Mitch gestured with the staple gun. "You'll notice the plastic, building-friendly clips I've already installed."

She stepped forward and craned her neck. "Oh."

"They won't work like that on the porch ceiling, so as a Christmas light professional, my choices are to drill holes, use adhesive and chance peeling off paint, or finesse with this nifty, low-powered staple gun made especially for installing Christmas lights."

"Oh."

"Not to worry." He took another sip. "You're not expected to know all the ins and outs of such a complex business."

She gave him the strangest look. She had to know he was kidding, right?

"Do you use that line on your financial clients?"

Where had that come from? "Of course not. In fact, the more my clients understand about their own portfolios, the easier it is for me."

"Hmm." Arms still crossed, she gazed up at him. "I would have thought it would be easier the other way around."

"What do you mean?"

"The clients who don't know anything—the ones who leave everything up to you. I'd think those would be your favorites."

How did they get from hot chocolate and Christmas lights to his clients? "I don't ever make decisions about a client's portfolio without conferring with that client. The less they know, financially, the more time it takes to explain and answer questions."

"But the less-savvy clients might not know to ask questions."

Mitch chugged the last of the cocoa and climbed down the ladder. "What's this about?"

She shrugged one shoulder. Elegantly. Even though he was suspicious, Mitch noticed.

"Just talking to you about your work. Though I must say if this is your reaction to questions, if I were a client, I wouldn't feel very encouraged to ask any."

"If you were a client, I wouldn't be standing on a ladder installing Christmas lights." He handed her the mug. "I'd be answering your questions."

She swirled the dregs of the cocoa. "Questions like, oh, say, what's Golden Boy Enterprises?" Her gaze latched onto his. She didn't smile.

"How did you find out about *that?*"

"Not an answer."

"Golden Boy Enterprises is our retirement account," he explained. "Jeremy and I set it up when we first got started."

"And conveniently located it offshore."

"Yes. To get experience with offshore accounts." He held her gaze so she'd know he was telling the truth. "We have clients who travel overseas and who have second and third homes in other countries. Having accounts outside the United States is convenient for them. And we have clients who want the privacy. GBE is one of several accounts we've set up over the years. Jeremy and I won't do business with an unfamiliar bank or corporation until we first give it a trial run with our own money."

"So you've got accounts all over the place."

So that's what this was about. She'd investigated him, which had to mean she was interested. Mitch grinned. "Don't sound so suspicious. We close them out once we're satisfied with the service, unless there's a reason to maintain an account in the country. We do have international clients."

"Oh." But she looked as though she had something else to say.

"Are we okay?" Mitch asked softly.

"Why Golden Boy? Why not Sloane and Donner?"

"It's our personal account. The name was Jeremy's idea."

"I should have guessed that."

"Also, we wanted to go through the process of filing a DBA—that's—"

"Doing Business As. I know."

He nodded. "Anyway, we wanted the experience of

filing as a foreign business. That's all. If we're going to make a mistake, we'd rather keep it in house."

"Makes sense, I guess."

Mitch tried to read her expression, but she was staring into his mug again. "I take it you've been investigating me."

"Well, duh."

"Find anything other than our offshore retirement account?"

A corner of her mouth crooked upward. "You have led a depressingly uneventful life."

He laughed. "It's hard to get into trouble when you spend all your time playing computer games. And then I went to college and studied. Okay, and played more computer games. And then Jeremy and I started our business—no more time for computer games—and I've been working ever since." That sounded pathetic. It *was* pathetic.

"When do you play?"

"I..." Don't. That was the truth. Honestly, he'd rather get all the long hours out of the way now so he could guarantee a more reasonable work schedule in a few years. "Getting established takes a lot of hours up front. Basically, I hit the gym to stretch out the kinks, grab something to eat, watch a little TV, sleep and start all over again. Not a whole lot of time for play." He gestured with the staple gun. "This is play." Could he possibly sound more like a drudge? Judging by Kristen's expression, no.

He tried to salvage the situation. "But hey, I'm taking a break on Friday when we're going out." He hoped they were still going out on Friday. "I'll pick the restaurant and you be in charge of the entertainment."

"I have a better idea." The Voice was back. She was practically purring. "I'll be in charge." She turned and undulated toward the door. "Of everything," she tossed over her shoulder.

MITCH HADN'T EXPECTED Kristen to dress in her film noir mode when they went out. Although he'd developed a true appreciation for the look, he was curious to see her dressed normally and if she still held the same fascination for him.

Mitch wasn't used to being fascinated by a woman. Attracted to, sure. Intrigued by, yeah. Unsure of, certainly. Lustful…hmm, that was memorable. He took a moment. Yeah. But fascinated? Not until Kristen. So he was curious when he rang the doorbell.

But he was stunned when the door opened.

"Hi." Black ringed her eyes and her red mouth had disappeared under a frosting of pale pink. And her hair was big. Bigger. Poufier. Sexy. Okay, he was onboard with that. The giant silver hoop earrings, not so much.

She had on a white tank top that revealed more than he'd seen looking down her blouse while on the ladder. Her short denim skirt settled around her hips leaving her stomach bare. And was that a belly ring? She looked like a cheerleader for the dark side.

There were a number of things he could have said at this point. "Wow, you look hot." That would have been okay and not too much, considering the skin factor. Or even just, "Wow." Even "Whoa, baby, come to Daddy," would have been better than what he actually said, which was, "Aren't you going to get cold?"

"I thought you'd keep me warm." It was The Voice, but it didn't sound right coming out of a frosty pink mouth.

He hesitated, trying to figure out what she expected of him.

"I guess not," she said and turned back inside.

Mitch was aware that he'd failed a critical test. Considering he'd passed an earlier test in spite of The Electric Santa truck and his red hoodie, he was confused.

And not dressed exactly right. He was going for upscale restaurant when he should have thought clubbing with a pair of those expensive dark wash jeans that fit oh so perfectly with just the right boot and a buttery soft leather jacket.

But no. He was wearing khaki chinos, a black golf shirt and a sport coat he'd borrowed from his father because he'd left his in Dallas. It fit. Mostly.

Oh, yeah. He was really stylin'.

Kristen returned with a black leather jacket draped over her arm. She handed the jacket to him as she locked the door.

When Mitch held it out to help her into it, she shook her head. "That's for you." She tugged off his tweed herringbone.

"This is your father's jacket," he said as he shrugged into it.

"Yes."

Oh, great. He abandoned any thoughts of a romantic "whatever" because the only thing worse than wearing his father's jacket was wearing *her* father's jacket.

"Much better." She draped his arm over her shoulders. "Isn't it?"

She was warm and soft and pressed up against him.

"Surprisingly, yes." A leather jacket was going straight to the top of his Christmas list.

They headed toward the driveway where his dad's SUV sat.

"Hey, no Santa-mobile!" she exclaimed.

"My parents wanted to drive it."

"They did not."

"Really. They have some parade meeting thing they're going to tonight and thought it would be funny."

"And you believed them."

"Well, yeah."

She nodded to herself. "Things are beginning to make more sense."

"What things?"

"You are very gullible."

Mitch opened the door for her, closed it and got in on the driver's side before answering her. "I am not gullible. You should have heard them laughing once they got the lights working. They drove about twenty miles an hour down the street and honked "ho ho ho" the entire time. The neighbor kids ran after them. But you're not talking about my parents and the truck. You're talking about Jeremy and me."

He flipped on the heater and the seat warmer.

"Possibly."

He felt her study him as he backed into the street. "So what's the verdict?"

"I can't totally figure you out yet," she said. "You're all-American on the outside, but maybe that's just a cover for a darker side."

The idea was so absurd that he laughed. "Or maybe what you see is what you get."

"In my experience, what I see is rarely what I get." Kristen squirmed until both nearly bare thighs were flush against the warm leather. "This is nice." She sighed. "One of those luxuries I'd like the opportunity to get used to. But back to you."

Mitch would have rather stayed with the naked skin and warm leather.

"Does having a dark side appeal to you?"

"No."

"No dark desires, hidden urges, or quirky curiosities?"

"Is that a line you read in an underground newspaper?"

"No, but it sounds pretty good, doesn't it?"

"The line, yes, the subject, no."

"Oh, come on." She leaned toward him ever so slightly and lowered her voice to a husky whisper. "Haven't you ever just *wondered*?"

Her voice invited him to confess, to share and possibly to satisfy. And he would have confessed and shared and wanted to satisfy—if there had been anything to confess or share. There was plenty to satisfy, but it wasn't what she had in mind.

Mitch was tempted to make something up when he thought about the movies he'd watched. "But it does fascinate me in a way." It did. Besides, he didn't want to sound totally bland, which is very much the way he felt he was coming off this evening.

"What way?"

"A warning way." He looked at her. "A film noir way."

Their gazes held. "That's an okay way," she said.

They had stopped at the light at the entrance to Kristen's neighborhood. She crossed her legs and—though Mitch didn't see how it possibly could—her skirt rose on her thighs. "Where are we headed?" he asked.

"Take a left and go to the freeway. Then we head north."

Toward Houston. "Into the big city it is."

As they drove through Sugar Land, Mitch pointed out jobs he'd done for The Electric Santa. When they passed the Town Square, he showed her where the company's giant stationary Santa Claus parade float would be. "I'll be working on it Christmas week. The light parade ends there and the rest of the floats will be on display." He gave a short laugh. "You could say I'm into the 'light side.'"

Kristen laughed politely, telegraphing her total disinterest in the "light side." She confirmed it with her next statement. "People who are drawn to the dark side fascinate me. What makes them go there? What's the appeal?"

"You're stuck on this tonight, aren't you?" Mitch merged onto the freeway. "What are we talking about, exactly? Dark side as in evil? Vampires?"

"More like Darth Vader dark side. Checking-morals-at-the-door dark side. Fun with a dash of depravity. Ever thought about letting go just once?"

Was she serious? If he weren't watching traffic, he'd look at her and try to read her expression. Jeremy would be able to tell what she was thinking without seeing her face.

"I have to say 'no.' None of that appeals to me."

"None?"

He shook his head. "Depravity doesn't do it for me. I'm pretty conventional." And he wasn't going to apologize for that, either.

"So...does that mean you don't like the way I'm dressed?"

Now there was a trick question. "I don't think you're dressed in a dark or depraved way."

She gave a low, throaty laugh that vibrated all the way through him. "I saw your face when I opened the door."

"That was surprise, not distaste."

There was silence. "You can follow that up with a compliment."

He smiled to himself. "What's a hot girl like you doing with a cool guy like me?"

She laughed. "You're about to find out. Take the next exit."

Richmond. The club scene. Mitch was not the club scene type. He knew this because he used to follow Jeremy around when they were still establishing themselves. Mitch didn't have a knack for when to absorb and when to discard the ever-changing trends. And the clubs Jeremy went to were all about trends. Mitch had to give his partner credit for recognizing an untapped demographic and within months, they had so many clients Mitch no longer had time to make the club scene.

He didn't miss it.

"Guess where we're going?" Kristen asked.

"A club?"

"But not just any club. I know the owner of this club."

Great. In spite of her father's leather jacket—*her father's leather jacket*—Mitch couldn't possibly win any comparisons to a club owner.

They reached the intersection. "Which way?"

"You don't know?"

No, and he was getting irritated. "Just tell me."

"Turn right."

The glitzy bars and restaurants quickly changed into a seedier area. The kind of area newly minted eighteen-year-old boys visited at least once.

"Well?" she asked.

"Well what?"

"Slow down! You'll miss the turn."

The only place she could be talking about was Tutti Fruitti. He turned anyway, and she didn't protest.

"Kristen, this is a strip club, not a bar club."

"I'll bet they serve drinks. And I know you could get a good table."

It appeared Miss Dark and Depraved didn't have any firsthand experience. What was up with her? The tires crunched over the shell parking lot and he parked on the outer edges. In the silence Mitch could feel the beat from the music thumping inside. "I'm not taking you in there. Especially since you look like you're here to audition."

She looked down at herself and gave a little shimmy. "I guess you'd know, since you own the place."

Chapter Six

"I've heard depravity can be a big money maker." Kristen thought she'd timed her bombshell nicely.

She'd subtly led up to it, setting the stage with her hoochie mama clothes and attitude and all the dark side talk.

Kristen was looking for a reaction. If Mitch had expressed a delighted surprise and the ever-important unchecked lustful gleam along with a significant attitude adjustment, then he'd have a difficult time convincing her he didn't know about the tangled nest of companies and where they led.

Another possibility was the deer-in-the-headlights look followed by sweaty palms, extreme discomfort and a slight stammer. Some people might think that would indicate that he'd have nothing to do with the adult entertainment industry, but Kristen had met this type and knew that such a man was even more likely to dabble.

Oh, and the crusaders. She'd nearly forgotten about those. The judgmental ones who secretly indulged.

Mitch's reaction was perfect. He was mildly puzzled at her persistence. Irritated, at the most. And he seemed willing to go with the flow, so he wasn't judgmental and he certainly wasn't threatened.

So that much was reassuring. She'd given him ample opportunity to drop his guard by letting him know she wasn't averse to a walk on the wild side, if that was what floated his boat.

But the ultimate test was taking him to one of the clubs. From his reaction, she didn't think he'd been here before, but that wasn't a requirement to own something. He didn't react to the name, as far as she could tell, so either he'd forgotten the names, or he truly had no idea of the clubs that were part of his holding company.

So, she'd dropped the bomb and it had exploded. And now she waited.

While she was waiting, she removed a stick of gum from her huge slouchy purse. She'd been unsure about smacking gum, but it seemed to fit her character. Or was that a cliché? She couldn't decide.

After a moment, Kristen caught herself chewing in time to the pulsing bass that throbbed through the car. The snap of the gum was annoyingly loud, mostly because Mitch hadn't said anything. She had not anticipated this reaction. Or lack of reaction. He seemed fascinated by the cars in the parking lot and the people coming and going into the club.

Kristen hoped he noticed that compared to some of the women, she looked conservative. Still, it was good to know that she got the look right. Sort of. A little more attitude and she'd be good to go.

Maybe he needed a nudge. She reached for the pack of gum and offered him a stick.

"Want some gum?" She met his gaze. "It's tutti-fruitti."

"Of course it is." His lips curled in secret amusement. "But no thanks."

He hadn't admitted or denied owning the place or even asked her what the heck she was talking about. Kristen zipped her purse. How to proceed? She needed a hint or a clue or something. "Shall we go in?" she asked when he continued to gaze out the windshield.

"Why?"

Good question. By this time, Kristen had expected she'd either be waltzing in on the arm of Mitch, the player, or explaining herself to Mitch, the stunned. "Uh, drinks?"

"And then what?"

"Food?"

"And then what?"

"Entertainment?"

He narrowed his eyes at her. "You find this sort of thing entertaining?"

Kristen carefully chose her words. "Men generally find this sort of thing entertaining."

"Only a certain type of man. *I*—" he paused for emphasis "—am not that type of man."

She lowered her voice to a sultry purr. "Well maybe I'm that type of woman." She inhaled and sucked in her stomach and was about to add pouty lips when Mitch had the gall to laugh.

"Trust me, you're not." And then he laughed again.

That stung. Certainly, she was playing against type, but he wasn't supposed to know that. "Is that your expert opinion?"

"I don't need to be an expert."

Kristen gasped.

"Don't choke on your gum." Mitch started the car.

"You...you—"

"It's all about drama with you, isn't it?"

"That is so not true. I am a calm, rational, realistic person."

"Who took me to a strip club for drag queens on a first date."

At that, Kristen did nearly swallow her gum. After waiting a second to see if he was kidding—nope—she turned around and stared through the rear windshield at the club clientele. Then she checked out the posters on the side of the building. Oh. By gumbies, he was right. Something she would have noticed if she hadn't been so intent on bombshell dropping. She turned back around. "Well, I don't like to be predictable."

"Predictability is not one of your problems." Mitch pulled a U-turn and headed back toward the ritzier section of Richmond.

"Are you saying I have problems?"

"Yes, but they're very attractive problems."

She knew he expected her to ask him what those problems were, but she wouldn't, not while he was ignoring the whole ownership-of-the-club issue.

"Where are we going?" she asked instead.

"To the nearest fast-food drive-through of your choice."

"What?"

He tossed a look her way. "You're not dressed for much else."

"So, you're, like, *punishing* me? Aren't you Mr. Prude." She crossed her arms and chewed her gum.

"This isn't a summer picnic in Sugar Land. It's a Friday night in December in an iffy part of Houston." He glanced over at her. "Nice pout by the way."

He was on to her. She might as well admit it. "Thanks. You don't think the lower lip is too much?"

"The lip is great. I'm not so sold on the gum."

"You know, I wasn't either. But when I found the tutti-fruitti flavor, I just had to go for it."

"Naturally." He made a snarky sound.

"Oh, get your mind out of the gutter." Kristen dug in her purse for the discarded wrapper and stuck the wad of gum into it. "I didn't fool you at all, did I?"

"You had your moments. And I applaud your choice of costume. Feel free to try out any more like that."

Kristen was slightly mollified. Okay, a lot mollified. But not if they were going to eat fast food. "Are you still going to make me eat fast food?"

Mitch waved negligently. "They all have salads now."

Oh, they did, did they? "Are you intimating that I *need* a salad?"

"Everybody should eat salad."

"While that is true, one doesn't usually head for monuments to grease and salt to buy one."

"I plan to go for the grease and salt, myself."

"Which you no doubt planned to eat in front of me after forcing me to order a bunch of lettuce?"

"Are you trying to pick a fight with me?" He didn't sound perturbed at all. If anything, he sounded highly entertained.

She'd lost her touch. Maybe she'd never had a touch.

Kristen needed a stronger reaction to play against. How was she supposed to work up any believable anger if Mitch wouldn't help her out? "It is very difficult to pick a fight with you. It's one of my best distracting maneuvers, too." She threw in a regretful sigh. "In this case, the plan was that if we got mad at each other, you'd take me home and I could get some real food."

He grinned and something—certainly not food—warmed in Kristen's middle.

"If you promise to wear your dad's jacket, I'll take you to a place with nice big booths and you can show me what you found out about me."

Deny or not to deny. That was the question. "What makes you think…" She trailed off as he rolled his eyes at her.

"Your purse—if you can call that thing a purse. I've got suitcases that are smaller. Anyway, your purse rustles. If there is one thing I know, it's the sound of paper rustling."

"Oh." So it was the props and not the acting. Yes, she'd stuffed her purse with printouts and notes and Web addresses. Since she wasn't sure what the significance of it all was she'd brought everything.

And Mitch didn't seem the slightest bit curious. If anything, he seemed amused. After the Tutti Fruitti incident, she could hardly blame him, but his lack of concern and utter faith in Jeremy worried her.

Without removing his hands from the steering wheel, Mitch indicated the dozens of restaurants and clubs lining Richmond Avenue as they drove past. "Do you see any place—"

"Tex-Mex!" Kristen pointed. "There. That one. It's

been forever since I've had good Tex-Mex food. It's just not the same in California." And, no, she wasn't just thinking of the sushi salsa place.

"I guess it wouldn't be," Mitch murmured as he turned into the restaurant parking lot.

"Mmm, *queso*. Chips. Salsa." She affected an accent. "Margareeeeetas."

"*Si, señorita.*" His accent was better than hers.

He'd probably paid attention in Spanish class.

Kristen inhaled the scent of peppers and cumin and fried onions when they got out of the car. "I'm thinkin' fajitas for two," she said.

"I'm thinkin' they'd better be at least half beef," Mitch said. "There is no such thing as a chicken fajita, I don't care what they say."

"Tell you what, if you spring for extra *queso*, we can order *all* beef."

"Deal." He shrugged out of the leather jacket. "I do believe you just managed to salvage this evening."

Unfortunately not for long, Kristen thought as she started toward the restaurant. Before they left, she had to convince him that he, well, that he owned a strip club for drag queens. How many margaritas would *that* take? She'd better plan on driving home.

"Hang on." Mitch caught up to her and draped the jacket over her shoulders.

"You were serious about me wearing the jacket inside?"

"Absolutely."

Kristen looked down at herself. "I know I've skipped a few crunches." She poked at her exposed stomach, which yielded alarmingly. "Okay, I've skipped a lot of crunches. But I didn't think I looked *that* bad." But definitely squishy.

Mitch pulled the edges of the jacket closed. They fell open again. He sighed. "You do not look bad. And you know it. But you do not fully appreciate how approachably hot you look. Men will want to approach. We do not want them to do that because then I would have to convince them to go away. But by this time, they will be gazing at you lustfully and will not want to go away. They will want to prove that they are the more worthy male by eliminating the competition—that would be me. Since I don't want to be eliminated, I would put up a good fight, but I'd rather eat fajitas and drink margaritas in peace."

She dismissed his words with a wave of her hand that sent the coat slithering off her shoulder. "You make everything too complicated. How 'bout I just kick 'em in the nuts?"

"How about you put your arms in the sleeves?"

He held the collar until she pushed her arms through the sleeves. Warmth—his warmth—settled around her making her feel protected and cherished. It was a nice change from the self-involved men she'd gone out with in Los Angeles. It hadn't mattered then because she'd been self-involved, too.

Kristen dipped her nose to the lining of the collar and breathed in the faint smell of shaving cream mixed with an earthier scent…cigar?

Kristen jerked her head up. Cigar. Her *father's* cigar. And probably her father's shaving cream, too. Ew. No. Not while she was having warm fuzzy feelings for

Mitch. Not good, not good. People went into therapy to get over less.

"Is it too late to change my mind about the dark side?" He lowered his voice suggestively. "You look like you're naked under that coat."

Her brain was going to explode.

"This is my father's coat. Thank you *so* much for saying that." Mitch was right, unfortunately. She could see her reflection in the window. Bare neck and miles of legs sticking out from the coat. Yeah. Her legs were still her best feature.

"I think it's pretty funny," he said, opening the door.

"No. No it's not. I tell you, I'm scarred for life."

Laughing, Mitch hung his arm across her shoulders in the universal she's-with-me signal.

As soon as they were seated in their booth, Kristen slipped out of the jacket, but wrapped the arms around her waist. She tossed her hair over her shoulder and noticed Mitch glaring at her. "What? I'm covered in leather from the waist down."

"I know." He briefly squeezed his eyes shut. "Try to look unapproachable. No eye contact with anyone but me."

"You mean like this?" She sent a smoldering look across the table.

And he sent a smoldering look right back. In fact, his smoldering look was better than *her* smoldering look and she'd been practicing.

Kristen was so surprised that he had a look like that in him that she blinked. She was pretty sure Mitch didn't. She was also pretty sure he saw her blink because one side of his mouth moved ever so slightly upward.

He had perfected the look of the confident, sexy male on the prowl.

Wait a minute. *She* was supposed to be the hottie here and he was supposed to be the befuddled nice guy. He was not supposed to be letting his smoking hot gaze drift from the top of her head all the way down her torso and back up again in a way that felt as though he was touching her.

And he *definitely* shouldn't have be able to add that slow, knowing smile.

Just then, their waiter thrust a red plastic basket of tortilla chips and a small bowl of salsa on the table, his arm right in the middle of their line of sight. It was excellent timing because Kristen didn't have a smoldering-look exit strategy. She'd never needed one before.

"Hello, my friends. What can I get you to drink this evening?"

"Two frozen margaritas with salt. She likes salt," Mitch said to the waiter.

He smiled as he scribbled their order. "And she is the type of woman a man wants to please, eh?"

Avoiding eye contact as instructed, Kristen bit into a chip as Mitch and the waiter exchanged a silent man-to-man thing before he left.

"I saw that," she said.

"What?"

"That way-to-go-amigo look he gave you."

Mitch looked pleased with himself. "Yeah, I liked that. It doesn't happen too often."

"Because I'm better looking than your usual dates?" Kristen preened a little.

Mitch dunked a chip in the salsa. "Because my usual dates wear more clothes."

"Oh, Mitch." Kristen shook her head in mock sympathy. "It's not the clothes. It's how they're worn."

"I see that now." He ate the chip and reached for another one. "Coverage and accessibility are very important. Low coverage, high accessibility. So noted."

Kristen should have been satisfied with the smoldering look.

As it happened, Mitch didn't have to fight off any men and Kristen nearly forgot the whole purpose of the evening. Okay, she didn't forget, she stalled. She stalled because she was enjoying herself more than she'd expected.

Mitch didn't resort to a canned patter or a schedule of date moves. Honestly, was there some book for men about dating that was making the rounds? First there was the head tilt with the enigmatic smile designed to prompt a "What?" or "Why are you looking at me like that?" The response would be a quiet compliment, followed by what Kristen liked to call a "rescue the puppy" story which was supposed to make the guy look good and the woman turn all gooey inside. Next came the touch—on the arm or leg, maybe even a heartfelt hand squeeze. After that came a series of maneuvers designed to create a romantic intimacy. Talking, listening, smiling, mirroring body positions and always at some point a faux shyness that somehow—and Kristen was never certain exactly *how*—led to a kiss. And other things. Why did the limpid look always work when she saw it coming a mile off?

There was no limpidness with Mitch. Neither did he respond to *her* date maneuvers, which, of course, she had and which, of course, she tried out—just to see what would happen. What happened, of course, was nothing.

Nothing turned out to be refreshing. Mitch was easy to be with. He talked, he listened and there was no pressure. Kristen didn't have to keep up the pretense of her successful career around him and he seemed very laid back and normal. Normal except for the SEC and the FBI investigating him.

Yeah, with guys there was always something.

Other than that, he was great date material.

They chit-chatted their way through an entire basket of chips, a bowl of queso just as decadent as she remembered, and half a frozen margarita—she was holding back—before Kristen reluctantly brought out the papers she had in her purse.

Yeah, the time had come and she was sorry. Pushing the chip basket aside and blotting condensation from their glasses with her napkin, Kristen smoothed the slightly crumpled papers into a stack.

Mitch stared at the stack. "You found that much stuff?"

"I only brought the relevant printouts."

"Relevant to what?"

Kristen looked into his eyes and didn't see the slightest suspicion. The guy truly had no idea. He honestly still thought the SEC and whoever had made a mistake.

He must have thought their trip to the club had been her idea of a joke. Kristen tried not to feel insulted because this was not about her and her abilities.

"I'm going to start at the beginning." She took his credit report from the stack. "I noticed that Anderson Personnel requested a credit report."

"Anybody can request a credit report."

"True, but it's usually because they plan to do business with you. So I checked them out." And then she showed him all the different holding companies Anderson Personnel was doing business as and what one of those companies owned. And then she showed him that his retirement fund owned Anderson Personnel. Therefore—

"I own a bunch of *strip* clubs?" His voice was loud enough to attract attention.

"Shh! We don't know that they're *all* strip clubs."

"Oh, come on! Look at those names."

Again with remarkable timing, the waiter appeared with their fajitas. Kristen hoped the sizzling meat on the metal plate had drowned out Mitch's horrified exclamation.

Judging from the waiter's sudden deference to Mitch and the speculative looks in her direction—no.

"But..." Mitch thumbed through the papers.

"I took the liberty of making a company family tree and all the DBA children." Kristen handed him another paper. "With colors."

He was clearly not impressed with the colors. "Where's Jeremy's name?"

"It wasn't there."

"But we both own Golden Boy."

"Not according to anything I came across." Kristen showed him copies of the DBA filings listing the legal owners. Mitch's name was there and Jeremy's was not. "It costs less than ten bucks to file a business name, so there could be dozens I didn't find."

Kristen decided she'd let Mitch absorb all this before she poured on part two.

While he absorbed, she'd eat fajitas. As she piled her tortilla with meat, onions, peppers, *pico de gallo* and sour cream, she wondered if Mitch would think she wasn't empathetic since she hadn't lost her appetite.

"Could you pass me the tortillas, please?"

Kristen took the lid off the tortilla keeper and held it out. "I was afraid you'd lost your appetite."

"I still might." He peeled a flour tortilla off the stack. "That's why I'm eating now."

"Good plan."

"There's more, isn't there?" And he wasn't talking tortillas.

Kristen met his eyes. "Have some sour cream."

They ate in silence. Mitch studied the papers and Kristen studied Mitch.

He concentrated fiercely on the information she'd given to him. Kristen figured he was looking for a flaw or an explanation or both. For his sake, she hoped he found one. She'd already decided that he was completely, even embarrassingly, innocent. A seasoned actor would be challenged to react as convincingly clueless.

She caught the eye of their waiter—not that hard to do—and ordered another margarita for Mitch.

He didn't seem to notice the exchange of glasses when he picked up the fresh one. "All right. Hit me with the rest of it."

Kristen waited until he'd taken a fortifying swallow. "The rest is Jeremy and his father, or at least Jeremy's father's land development company."

Mitch nodded as he carefully set his glass in the wet ring it had made. "He's referred some of his clients to us. That's not illegal. They know Jeremy is his son."

"Right, but here's where it gets complicated."

Mitch pushed aside the remains of his dinner. "I thought we'd already done complicated."

"Not like this." Kristen showed him lists of investment trades, the companies making them, properties bought and sold and their selling prices and who was doing the buying and selling.

"That's a lot of activity, but, here again, nothing illegal."

"Ah." Kristen had printed some of the details on pale green paper. "This information is courtesy of my mother." Kristen held the papers close to her chest before letting Mitch see them. "It's confidential to real estate professionals. In fact, if it hadn't been for my mom—and my dad, too—"

"Your *parents* know?"

"Well, yeah. How did you think I got access to all this info?"

"Great. That means *my* parents are going to know." He took a large swallow of margarita and winced. "Brain freeze."

"Ouch." Kristen made a sympathetic face even though she was the one with the melted dregs in her glass because she wanted to remain sharp and capable of driving home in case Mitch was one of those men who liked to drown his sorrows. "My parents won't say anything because of client confidentiality."

"I'm not a client."

"But *I* am. I hired myself."

Mitch looked a question at her as he dug in the basket for any leftover chip crumbs.

"The Dater's Special. We do background checks for people—mostly women—who want to make sure the guys they're involved with are who they say they are and there aren't any current wives or heavy-duty child support payments or felonies they neglected to mention."

"Nice. But I disclosed everything. Everything I knew, anyway."

"I wanted a legit paper trail in case there's any question about why I investigated you. Anyway, the information on these papers came from my mom's contacts and isn't going into the files."

"Gotcha."

Kristen handed him the green papers.

Mitch stared at them. "What am I looking at?"

"Lots of your clients' money seems to find its way into real estate before ending up elsewhere. My mother is plugged into a group that chats about sales and experiences that are out of the norm." Kristen gestured as she tried to explain. "She *won't* tell me any more."

He flipped through the pages. "So how does this affect me?"

"For whatever reason, these property sales attracted attention. And, oh, look, they all involve Sloane Property Development and Construction. And you. In technical terms, your little family of DBAs is hanging out with Jeremy's dad's big family of DBAs. Something's not right about that. I know it. I *feel* it."

Mitch looked up at her. After a long moment, he slowly nodded. "Okay."

"I thought it would help if I followed one trail all the way from the beginning—you, or rather an investment your company made on behalf of a commercial client." Kristen pulled out a chart that she'd taped together.

Mitch didn't know it, but he was looking at two

days of her life. Honestly, with all the names, it was like following an ant through an anthill.

"I remember that." Mitch pointed to the beginning of the chart. "He's one of Chuck Sloane's referrals."

"My mother has serious issues with that guy."

"Jeremy's father?"

"Yeah. She's gone head-to-head with him on some real estate deals and hasn't been very happy about the way things turned out. She said he has an uncanny knack for buying and selling worthless property which then isn't worthless anymore and inflates the property taxes in the area."

"Hmm."

Mitch had tuned her out to concentrate on her chart. "May I write on this?"

She nodded, but he didn't look up. "Go ahead."

He brought out a mechanical pencil and a fancy shmancy electronic phone thingie like she'd never been able to afford.

"Blackberry?"

"Palm Treo. I was allowed to keep it since all the files were in my computer anyway." He still didn't look at her, not that she was trying to get him to do so. She was interested in watching him, waiting for a reaction or at least an explanation. She felt entitled after all the hours she'd spent researching and making herself dizzy with numbers.

Besides, he was much easier on the eyes than numbers.

Minutes passed and Kristen began to notice details in Mitch's face that she'd missed before. Details like the way the short hairs right in front of his ears grew in different directions. Details like the shape of his ear lobes, the bump in the bridge of his nose and the length of his eyelashes. There were a couple of tiny scars—one near the outer edge of his eye and the other on his chin. The crease between his eyebrows deepened when he concentrated. It was attractive now, but in ten years, he'd want to Botox it.

His face was nicely shaped, but his cheekbones weren't angular enough to look good on camera. And if she were doing a makeover on him, she'd part his hair on the other side, or give him one of those short shaggy cuts with lighter brown streaks in the front.

She imagined him with various styles of facial hair. No mustache because his lips were very well shaped. She couldn't see him in a full beard, either. A goatee? Maybe. Maybe not. Ick on a soul patch. He could wear his sideburns longer, though. A little bronzer wouldn't be amiss, either. His eyebrows could be tamed a bit.

There was some seriously good raw material here.

Rough up a few of his edges…and now that she thought about it, he was just *made* for the stubble look, except that was losing popularity, which was fine with her because kissing stubble was bad for the skin.

His jaw clenched. Kristen looked down and saw his finger at the place on the chart where the money trail began to loop back on itself. Companies were investing in themselves, but were losing money. Kristen hadn't been able to figure that one out, either. And she was no expert, but it didn't look good to have Mitch taking clients' money and investing in his own company. He'd discover that info after he moved his finger another three inches. If he was clenching his jaw now, he'd be steaming when he got to that part.

Kristen became impatient. She'd waved their waiter away twice, but was rethinking a second margarita.

She shifted, peeling her thighs off the booth's vinyl seat.

It couldn't be long before Mitch realized he'd been betrayed by his partner and Kristen wanted to catch his expression at the precise moment he realized it.

Betrayal was such a powerful action and elicited an equally powerful emotion. Kristen had never been betrayed on the level Mitch was going to experience. Sure, she'd been fooled and disappointed, but she'd never been blindsided.

This was an opportunity for her to see genuine emotion and remember exactly how it looked so when she was called upon to portray it, she'd be able to do so convincingly.

Mitch's finger moved slowly across the page and he seemed to recalculate or look something up every few seconds.

Hurry up already! Kristen was afraid to blink in case she missed something.

But Mitch blinked. Repeatedly. He must have seen the part where the money ended up back in one of his own shell businesses.

Kristin watched closely. But he said nothing.

Blinking? That was it? Huge betrayal equals blinking?

She could do blinking. In fact, she tried it, but there should be more.

Mitch's chest rose and fell and Kristen thought she heard the faintest catch. That was when she realized that there *was* more to Mitch's reaction. His face had paled, but due to the festive ambient lighting—beer advertisements and chili pepper lights—she hadn't noticed. Sweat appeared on his upper lip. Okay, she couldn't do that, but the breath thing was good.

And then he raised his eyes to hers and her breath caught for real.

Pain. Deep pain. There was no life in his eyes, which dominated his face. They were huge and dark and his skin was putty-colored in between flashes of the blinking red-and-yellow neon beer sign.

But his eyes would always haunt her. Such overwhelming pain in them. No denial, no bitterness, no anger—not yet.

Just soul-searing pain.

Kristen was deeply disgusted with herself. How could she have treated Mitch's feelings as an acting tutorial? Looking at his face made her stomach queasy.

She wanted to ease the pain, but what could she say? What was there to say? The only good thing about this was that as awful he felt, Mitch now knew the truth and could take steps to protect himself.

Chapter Seven

The silence stretched until Kristen couldn't stand it. "I'd hoped I was wrong," she finally murmured. Mitch probably didn't hear her.

But he must have picked up the sentiment because he closed his eyes, inhaled and tilted his chin slightly.

When he opened his eyes, his expression had hardened. Anger and self-loathing had mixed with the pain. "I've been a prize-winning, gold-medal sucker."

"No—" Kristen started.

"Yes. When I look at you, I see pity. Just what every red-blooded man wants to see in the eyes of a hot *chiquita.*"

"That's not pity. It's empathy."

"Sure, it is." His mouth twisted. "I suppose you got a good laugh out of this."

"I never laughed and I never felt like laughing." Kristen hoped this wasn't going to turn into a kill-the-messenger situation.

"I'll bet Jeremy's laughing."

"We already know Jeremy's a jerk."

"He must not be able to believe his luck. He got a

partner who did all the grunt work and never thought to check up on him. When Jeremy came up with some idea that stretched legal boundaries or even *appeared* dicey, I'd tell him why we shouldn't do it. Sure, he'd grumble, but we either compromised or he'd agree to drop it. It never occurred to me to make sure he did." Shaking his head, Mitch stared at the papers spread in front of him. "How stupid was that? Stupid, stupid, incredibly stupid."

Kristen signaled their waiter. "I'm ordering you another margarita."

"I don't want another margarita."

"It'll numb the sting. I'll drive."

"Oh, this is so much more than a sting. This is a stab in the back." Mitch illustrated with the table knife.

"Another margarita," Kristen said as the waiter approached. "And hurry."

"Cancel that," Mitch snarled.

She turned to him. "Mitch…"

"Tequila shot. Limes," he ordered.

Well, all right then. "Efficiency is good." She wondered if he'd actually ever drunk a tequila shot before.

Mitch slumped against the padded vinyl back of the booth and stared at her across the table.

Kristen was encouraged to see that the raw pain in his eyes had been replaced by anger. Fortunately, it wasn't the boiling-over-punch-the-wall-and-break-a-hand anger. She imagined he was mentally reviewing everything he'd been doing lately and looking at Jeremy's activities through a different lens.

"You don't have to babysit me," he said.

"I'm a designated driver. Not a babysitter."

The waiter rushed over with a shot glass of tequila, salt and a dish of limes. "Wait," Mitch instructed.

Deftly, he licked his hand, poured salt on it, licked it off, downed the shot and bit into a lime wedge. "Another one and make it El Tesoro Platinum this time. I don't want a hangover."

"*Si, señor.*" The waiter actually bowed.

Kristen raised an eyebrow. This was an interesting development. It appeared that Mitch wasn't as blandly vanilla as she'd thought. Good to know.

Mitch resumed staring at her, all affability gone from his expression. His eyes were harder, his jaw was set and his slouch gave off a sullen vibe.

There was no bewildered whipped-puppy air about him.

The man had been done wrong and he was barely containing his rage. "So tell me what the club bit was all about earlier."

"Just making sure your hands were clean," Kristen told him.

He made a disgusted sound and reached for the salt and lime when he saw the waiter approach. "I'm flattered you thought I had enough brain power to be involved." He picked up the tequila shot directly from the tray before the waiter could set it on the table. Slamming this shot back with the same smooth proficiency as the first, he returned the glass to the tray and waved away a third.

And how hot was that? Hot enough that Kristen wished she were sitting on the same side of the booth so she could kiss some of that salt and lime and tequila and tongue into her mouth. Oh, yeah. Mr. Vanilla Nice Guy had left the building. This guy was pure Rocky Road.

She was supposed to be taking a break from the aptly named Rocky Road types. She was not supposed to be listening to the immature part of her that found brooding bad boys appealing.

But Mitch wasn't a bad boy. He was a nice guy with experience. Hey, a new combo. She liked it. A lot. How messed up was that? Mitch's life had blown up in his face and Kristen found his reaction hot.

This was so not about her.

Except he was looking at her. No, *looking* wasn't the right word.... Watching? Waiting? For what? For her to say something? Do something? If he kept staring at her that way, she was going to crawl across the table and—

"I'm in real trouble," he finally said.

At least he acknowledged it. Kristen made herself ignore his hotness factor and be supportive. "That's what lawyers are for. And at least you'll be able to provide this information so—"

"I am in real trouble because no one will believe that I could have been so stupid." He grimaced in disgust.

"Please stop beating yourself up."

"I'm not beating myself up."

"Then stop using the word *stupid*."

"Kristen." Mitch straightened and leaned forward, lacing his fingers together on top of the table. His knuckles were white. He spoke slowly as though lecturing a child. "Even the most junior bank teller is trained to recognize this. I have a masters degree in business and accounting. I'm half owner of a company that invests and manages other people's money. I have years of experience. There is no government investigator, no jury, no judge anywhere who will believe that I was totally unaware of what's going on."

He was mad. She got that. But he needed to ditch the patronizing attitude. "Well, I'm not a bank teller. And I never finished college," Kristen snapped. "So do you suppose you could tell *me* what's going on? Use little words."

Mitch's expression didn't change. "Money laundering."

Kristen had visions twentieth-century gangsters in baggy pinstriped suits. "For real?"

He nodded.

"How do you know?"

"All the activity and the shell companies. The whole point of money laundering is to hide cash that comes from crime and make it appear as though it was legitimately earned. This—" he waved at the papers "—is the ideal setup. Yeah." He stared at Kristen's chart. "Perfect."

"Show me."

Mitch stood and came over to her side of the booth. Kristen slid over to make room, sighing for the lost tequila-salt-lime-tongue opportunity. The mood was so over.

"Okay." He turned the papers around to face them. "There're three parts to money laundering—placement, which is getting the excess cash into the system, layering, where it's mixed all around with legit money, and integration, where it can be withdrawn without attracting suspicion."

"There are three parts and they're named?"

"Oh, yeah. Underground money is a huge problem. There are organizations and Web sites devoted to fighting money laundering. Annual conferences are held all over the world."

"I didn't realize." And it sounded as though Mitch was in worse trouble than she thought.

"Anyway, say you're a crook and you've got a whole lot of cash. It attracts attention you don't want. So you look for businesses where a lot of cash is used like casinos, restaurants, bars—"

Kristen gasped. "Strip clubs! Think of all the tips."

"Exactly. Oh, and banks or, say, *financial services firms*."

"Omigod." Kristen was getting the picture and it wasn't pretty.

"But financial institutions are trickier to use because you need somebody on the inside. Or even better, somebody who can be fooled into being a cash conduit."

"And that was you."

He nodded. "Apparently so. Except I would have been suspicious if a client had handed me a suitcase of cash, so I wasn't the entry point. I just sent the money into the machine to be washed."

"How?"

"I'd set up an account. I'd make some legit investments, as I always do. But the client can also make deposits and withdrawals." Mitch pointed to the twisted trail of companies. "They'd transfer money here and shift it around so many times that no one could ever trace it." He ran a finger along Kristen's chart. "Here you didn't really follow one sum of money. What you did was link the shell companies that did business with each other."

"Oh." There went two days of her life.

"Hey." He nudged her with his shoulder. "You did good."

"Thanks." She nudged him back. "So what about Jeremy's dad? Does he know?"

Mitch looked down at her, his expression grim. "What do you think?"

"Just considering my mother's reaction, I'd have to say guilty, guilty, guilty."

"I'd say that, too, because guess what's one of the favorite ways to get money back out of the system?"

"Well, it's got to be something to do with real estate."

"Buying and selling property. Lending money to buy and sell property." Mitch folded the chart. "Big ticket stuff. The sales price is recorded on the county tax roles for anybody to see all nice and legal. And so the money is back from the cleaners."

Mitch continued to gather the papers as Kristen struggled to understand. "So...this isn't like a one-time thing."

"Oh, no."

"It was a setup."

"And a good one." Mitch handed her the papers and then inexplicably salted a lime wedge and bit into it.

"You can order—"

"No." He signaled the waiter for the check, reached for his wallet and tossed some bills on the table.

It was a generous tip. Mitch probably earned less than the waiter.

"Let's go." Mitch dropped his keys into Kristen's hand.

Suddenly liking him very, very much, she squeezed her fingers around them.

"BUT WHY DOES JEREMY need to launder money?" Kristen asked. She'd asked lots of questions. Questions that made Mitch think. He was tired of thinking.

"Because it's very profitable." He got in the passenger side of the car and slammed the door.

Kristen walked around to the driver's side and got in, flashing lots of leg as she did so. "But where did he get the money to launder?"

"I don't know. Just start the car!"

She gave him a look that was withering and poutily sexy at the same time.

The tequila had quenched the burning fires of rage—and also colored Mitch's thoughts with overwrought drama.

The tequila had not quenched the burning fires for Kristen, which had ignited back when she'd opened the door to her house. If anything, it had fanned those flames.

As though he had any chance with her at all now.

He didn't know for sure, but he had the impression that dating her would be problematic while he was in jail.

And it was all thanks to his buddy, his pal, his one-time roommate, his partner, his amigo, Jeremy.

At least now he could think the name without danger of rupturing a blood vessel.

Mitch hadn't known he was capable of such anger—a lot of which had been directed at himself. Jeremy shouldn't have been able to fool him and now Mitch was taking his anger out on Kristen.

This would be the same Kristen who was his only ally. The Kristen who had spent untold hours digging around when he'd been stringing Christmas lights and waiting for Jeremy to fix everything.

Oh, he'd fixed everything all right.

Mitch stared across the car at Kristen and forced himself to inhale and exhale deeply.

He should have drunk more tequila because as much of a mess as he was in and in spite of knowing that she had been pretending tonight, she was still wearing an outfit that revealed a whole lot of skin, which he liked. The skin and the outfit.

Kristen signaled and merged onto the freeway. "Has that tequila kicked in yet?"

"As much as it's going to."

"Feeling any better?"

"I will after I apologize for snapping at you."

"It's okay."

"Not really." Mitch rubbed his eyes. "I haven't even thanked you. You spent hours on this, Kristen."

"I sure did. And don't think I won't remind you when I need a favor some time, like when I'm rich and famous and need someone to handle all my money."

"I'm not going to be doing any favors from jail."

"Are you giving up?"

"Nah. I'll go through the motions, but..." He made an *L* with his fingers and pressed his forehead. "Loser."

"Hey! I don't hang out with losers. Oh." She grimaced. "Okay, I'm not going to hang out with losers anymore, starting right now. With you."

"Great. Now I'm a charity project."

"I'm not that altruistic. I'm with you because I want to be."

Sure she was. "So you're saying that dumb, gullible, number geeks appeal to you?"

"Now you're just being morose. It's not attractive."

"Too bad, 'cause there's a lot more morosity where that came from."

Kristen grinned. "*Morosity* isn't a word."

"So what? Are the language police going to send me to vocabulary jail?"

"You have now moved on to petulance. I'm not seeing that as an improvement."

"I wasn't trying to improve. There's no point."

"And depression makes an appearance."

"Kristen, this is not an emotions quiz. You don't have to identify each one."

"But you're going through them so fast."

"Not as fast as you drive. Wanna back it off a little?"

He expected an objection, but didn't get one. Kristen eased her foot off the accelerator.

There was silence, blessed silence in the car. But that meant he could think and his thoughts weren't pleasant. "I never suspected anything. I wonder how long...when it all started. I saw Jeremy every day. How many of those days did he look me in the eye and lie to me? I have no idea. He's the same Jeremy he's always been. We even shared an apartment for four years! How could he do this to me? And why did I never sense this about him?"

He looked over at Kristen. "You're not saying anything."

"No."

"Smart girl."

We'd like to send you two free books to introduce you to our brand-new line – Kimani Romance™! These novels feature strong, sexy women, and African-American heroes that are charming, loving and true. Our authors fill each page with exceptional dialogue, exciting plot twists, and enough sizzling romance to keep you riveted until the very end!

KIMANI ROMANCE ... LOVE'S ULTIMATE DESTINATION

Your two books have a combined cover price o[f] $11.98 in the U.S. and $13.98 in Canada, but are yours **FREE!** We'[ll] even send you two wonderful surprise gifts. You can't lose

2 Free Bonus Gifts!

Two NEW Kimani Romance™ Novels
Two exciting surprise gifts

I have placed my Editor's "thank you" Free Gifts seal in the space provided at right. Please send me 2 FREE books, and my 2 FREE Mystery Gifts. I understand that I am under no obligation to purchase anything further, as explained on the back of this card.

168 XDL EF2K 368 XDL EF2V

FIRST NAME LAST NAME

ADDRESS

APT.# CITY

STATE/PROV. ZIP/POSTAL CODE

Thank You!

Please allow 4 to 6 weeks for delivery. Offer limited to one per household and not valid to current subscribers of Kimani Romance. All orders subject to approval. Credit or debit balances in a customer's account(s) may be offset by any other outstanding balance owed by or to the customer.

"Yes."

He smiled, surprised he still could.

He stared out the window as the big city lights of Houston faded from view and the flat land opened up.

So now what? Jeremy had set him up but good. The guy was smarter than Mitch had given him credit for. Or his dad had helped him. Or both.

If Mitch reported his suspicions to the police or the FBI, they'd just figure he was trying to save himself. Which he would be. But it was such a sweet system. They'd never believe he had no clue. Even he couldn't believe he'd had no clue, no inkling, no suspicion. And the way Jeremy had become the front man and left Mitch with all the technical details—pure brilliance. Jeremy would act shocked. His father was a respected small-town businessman. *He* would act shocked. They were good with people. They'd know just the right things to say.

And they'd had weeks to practice. Weeks to clean up. Weeks to make Mitch look guilty.

He couldn't count on help from the FBI. They thought they had their man—him.

This was one time when doing the right thing would be the wrong strategy.

Kristen took the Sugar Land exit off the freeway. As she turned to go beneath the overpass the dingy shadows and concrete reminded Mitch of the black-and-white films he'd been watching. "That's it," he said. "I'm living a film noir. You're the femme fatale. I'm the doomed patsy."

"Mitch, will you please get over yourself?"

"It's true. A favorite theme is the innocent man being

framed and trying to prove it. He has to fight both the bad guys *and* the good guys."

"So what happens?"

"Somebody usually gets shot."

"I nominate Jeremy."

"No." Mitch straightened. "That won't do it. I need to clear my name. I need revenge. And I need for Jeremy to realize that he's not as clever as he thinks he is."

"And that you're not as stupid as he thinks you are." She nodded. "I get it."

"We're not using the *s* word. But, yes. That, too." He looked over at her. "If I'm going to get him, Kristen, I'll need your help. You in?"

She flashed him a huge grin. "I am *so* in."

Chapter Eight

Kristen rested her chin on her hand and looked through the doorway of her father's office to where Mitch sat at her desk.

She'd driven directly here once Mitch had decided to fight back. She hadn't wanted to chance him sleeping on it and changing his mind.

In an ideal world, he could go to whatever entity was in charge of catching money launderers. This was not an ideal world. Kristen knew that. And Mitch pointed out that even if it was established that he'd been completely unaware, who would want to hire a money manager who hadn't known that his own portfolio was being used in money laundering?

So this was both personal and professional with him.

But it was three a.m. and they still didn't have a plan. They were gathering information. Okay, fine. But Kristen was bored. Yes, she knew what was at stake. She was still bored. This was the tedious part they skipped in books and movies.

Her assignment had been to investigate Jeremy's father and his company to find anything Mitch could use.

Kristen smothered a yawn. Where was the glamour? The excitement? The hot sex?

That would wake her up.

Not that she was in the mood right now, but Mitch didn't know that. He could at least try something. When she said she'd help him, she'd meant it, sure, but she'd expected some breaks where he felt moved to express his gratitude. And she would feel moved to express her, um, gratitude for his gratitude. But he hadn't made eye contact with her, not even when she'd spoken directly to him.

He'd lost his mojo, that's what had happened. He was embarrassed.

He had no reason to be, as far as Kristen was concerned. He'd trusted. Jeremy was scum. And son of scum.

Kristen stretched her arms over her head. She needed to plug Mitch's testosterone leak before he became a mere shell of a man. It was the right thing to do.

"I'm getting tired," she announced, her arms still over her head.

No response.

"And my back and shoulder are aching." She arched her back and held it until the muscles started to cramp.

He didn't look up.

Oh, come on. That had been a great pose. His peripheral vision should have alerted him.

Maybe she was too late and he was nothing but a husk of a man. This called for emergency resuscitation.

She got up and approached him. "Want a bottle of water? Coffee?"

He gazed at the monitor. "I'm good."

Kristen walked behind his chair and deliberately placed her hands on his shoulders. His muscles tensed. "I figured if my shoulders hurt, yours must, too." She pressed with her thumbs and kneaded with her fingers, really going after the knots.

He allowed it for a few brief seconds and then tried to shake her off. "Thanks. I'm fine."

"You are not fine." Kristen yanked the rolling chair out from the desk, spun it around and sat in his lap.

"Kristen!" After a brief surprised look, he fixed his gaze over her shoulder. "What are you doing?"

"Mitch." She touched his jaw. "Look at me."

He jerked his jaw away, but met her eyes.

Nope. No mojo there. She shifted on his lap. No mojo anywhere. "Mitch, being set up like this could have happened to anyone."

"But it didn't. It happened to me."

How could she convince him? "I don't want you thinking that I look down on you or anything."

"Okay. Thanks. We should get back to work."

A girl could get a complex. "Mitch, I..." This was so difficult when he gazed at her with all the expression of a statue. "I'm trying to say that this...situation doesn't make you any less attractive."

His eyes shifted to that place over her shoulder again.

"If anything it makes you even more appealing because...because you were in a relationship. You committed yourself to your friendship and to making that relationship work. And you trusted completely. Jeremy counted on that trust; otherwise he wouldn't have been able to work the scam. *He* betrayed *you*. *He* should feel ashamed. But don't count on it because anybody who could court your trust knowing that he intended to break it is not a normal human being."

He was looking at her again—warily, but at least he could face her.

"But you—you trusted. You *committed*. You stayed loyal until the evidence was overwhelming. Women are desperate to find a guy like you." She gazed into his eyes. "*I'm* desperate to find a guy like you."

And she leaned down and kissed him. She'd meant the kiss as a kind of exclamation point to her speech, a reassurance that he was still an attractive man.

She hadn't intended to linger and she certainly hadn't planned on melting into him—at least not this time. But melt she did.

Maybe it was the angle, since she was sitting on his lap and had to bend down. Maybe it was the way her hair fell softly forward, curtaining their faces. Maybe it was because she'd initiated the kiss. Maybe it was everything that kept her lips on his.

Or it could have been because Mitch grabbed her arms as if he'd planned to push her away from him and ended up circling his hands around her back and moving one up to fist a handful of her hair.

Yeah, that was probably it.

The man kissed as though he were starving for it. As though he thought she'd never kiss him again. It was a chaste, but strangely intense kiss.

He needed more reassurance, that was it. Kristen settled her torso more firmly against his chest, the shift in weight causing the chair to rock back. Mitch's hand was now splayed over her bare midriff. He brushed his fingers against her skin, making her shiver even as the warmth spread.

She moved her mouth softly, but insistently over his, savoring the sensations, taking her time, letting him know there was no rush and she wasn't going anywhere.

It took several moments before Kristen felt Mitch relax—not that she was complaining. She rubbed his chest, her fingers exploring his muscles, and moved her hand up to cup his jaw. Urging his lips open, she tasted hints of salt and lime before stroking his tongue with hers.

She was totally driving this kiss. However, as the driver, it was up to her to let him know where they were going.

The thing was, Kristen had been driving aimlessly, so to speak. Not that the ride hadn't been fun—was still fun—but it was time to put the car back into the garage.

She gave a tiny, contented little "mmm" and ended the kiss, pulling back slowly.

Very nicely done, if she did say so herself. Maybe she'd gone a little overboard, but she didn't expect Mitch to complain.

His eyes were still closed as she moved back and he was smiling faintly. Ha. Mission complete. Mojo restored. She looked forward to next time when he might put some of that mojo to good use.

Speaking of…he hadn't said anything. She waited.

Slowly, his eyelids lifted. She tried to read his expression, but couldn't.

"That was one hell of a pity kiss."

Kristen straightened and removed his hand from her

back. "That wasn't a pity kiss. Pity kisses get less tongue." She pushed herself off his lap, not caring if she squashed his leg in the process.

If he was so determined to feel sorry for himself, then he just could. She turned around to tell him so, but caught the quick flash of humor in his eyes and remained silent.

Humor was good. He'd be okay.

"I HAVE A PLAN." Mitch's voice sounded from above her.

Kristen had fallen asleep on the leather loveseat, flat on her back, her knees crooked over the arm. She opened her eyes and saw that Mitch was holding a Starbucks sack.

"Does your plan involve coffee?"

"Absolutely. Scoot over."

Kristen rearranged herself as Mitch sat and handed her a venti something. "I don't suppose this is a decaf skim-milk latte?"

He snorted in disgust and sipped his coffee. "No."

"Oh, thank goodness." She drank deeply and felt the whole milk fat molecules slip over her tongue. Wonderful. Fabulous. "What are you drinking?"

"Espresso. Quad shot."

"You'll never sleep again."

"Like I have time." He shook the bag. "I have a scone thingie, a muffin and something gooey."

"You wonderful man." Kristen went for the muffin. "So what's your plan?"

He was staring at the muffin in her hand, so Kristen broke off a piece and fed it to him.

"My plan," he said when he'd swallowed, "is to get

Jeremy to dirty his hands." He snitched another piece of her muffin. "With me gone, there's got to be a backlog."

"He'll claim that you set everything up and he was just executing trades that you'd started." She took a bite of muffin before Mitch ate it all.

"I thought of that. So he'll have to set up a new account all by himself."

Mitch watched Kristen's mouth the way a cat watches a piece of string. It was so cute; Kristen relented and gave him the rest of the muffin.

"How does that prove that you're innocent?" She reached for the bag and pulled out the scone. The gooey thing looked interesting, but it was a little early and she'd had too little sleep.

"It doesn't, but it proves that he knew what was going on."

"And this helps you how?" Kristen broke off a piece of scone and popped it into her mouth.

"It establishes reasonable doubt."

Kristen ate another piece and waited. "That's it? That's your plan?"

"So far." He reached for her scone and she smacked his hand away, then immediately relented and gave him a big hunk of it.

"So how are you going to get Jeremy to set up the account?"

"I don't know," he said around a mouthful of scone.

"You don't have much of a plan."

"Not yet. I figured you and I could brainstorm the details."

He was so upbeat—although that could be the caffeine—Kristen couldn't discourage him.

"Don't forget about Jeremy's father," she said.

"I haven't, but first things first."

Kristen brushed the crumbs off her fingers, grabbed her coffee cup and stood. "I don't think you can bring one down without bringing down the other. They've probably got safety nets in place for both of them. If it were me, I'd stash money outside the country and take off at the first sign of trouble."

"But they didn't—Kristen, you're a genius!" He leaped to his feet and hugged her.

Which was the exact moment the door opened and Kristen's father walked in. "Good morning." His gaze swept the two of them. "Here to finish the lights, Mitch?"

"I already finished, Mr. Zaleski. Kristen and I were working on something else."

"So I see." He hung his jacket on the coat rack.

Kristen had been trying to hide behind Mitch without looking as though she was trying to hide behind Mitch. "What are you doing here, Dad? It's Saturday."

"I'm trying to get caught up so I can take a couple of days off at Christmas."

"That makes sense."

"I thought so." Her father smiled as an awkward silence fell.

At least it was awkward for Kristen, who chanted silently to herself, *I'm an adult, I'm an adult* even as she positioned her arms to cover her belly ring.

Mitch cleared his throat. "Kristen tells me you helped research my…my…"

"Money laundering problem?" her father smoothly supplied.

"You knew?" Kristen asked.

"I suspected. I've had experience with people trying to hide assets in divorce cases. They've got the shell companies and the offshore accounts just as you found. Not on such a large scale, though," he added.

"Mr. Zaleski, I want to assure you that as difficult as it is to believe, I had no knowledge of any of this before Kristen showed me what she'd found."

"It's true," Kristen said. "I followed my hunch," she threw that in because she knew her dad liked hunches, "and went undercover to a…club. With Mitch. That he owns. But didn't know he owned." She should stop right now.

"You're not under much cover from what I can see," said her father and headed toward his office.

Kristen threw Mitch a "help me" look.

"We came back here to see what else we could find out," he said.

Kristen's father turned in the doorway. "And?"

"You better sit down, Dad."

He sat, but he made them call Mitch's parents and Kristen's mother first. Mitch protested, but Kristen knew her father well enough to recognize that this was not a negotiable point.

An hour later, everybody had been brought up to speed.

"Carl, I'm glad you insisted that Mitch call us," Patsy Donner said. "Mitch, I can't believe you were trying to deal with this on your own."

"I didn't want to worry you. But honestly," he exhaled, "I'm glad you know now."

"I should think so," Patsy said.

"To be fair, Mitch didn't know there was anything to worry about until yesterday," Kristen said.

Mitch's father leveled a look at him. "Call me overly cautious, but if the FBI and the SEC impounded all my possessions and froze my accounts, I'd consider it cause for concern."

"I thought they'd made a mistake," Mitch explained. Again. "Let's move on."

"They haven't made their case yet, or Mitch wouldn't still be walking around," Kristen's father offered. "They don't have the advantage of Barb making the real estate connection, which is pure, genuine, one-hundred-percent luck."

"I knew it. I *knew* there was something off with that smug Chuck Sloane." Barbara Zaleski had been pacing nearly the whole time because she had been too incensed to sit still. "More than once, I'd get a really good offer on a piece of junk property and he'd swoop in at the last minute and pay a little more. My client would be thrilled until Sloane would turn around and sell the property the next week for twice what he'd paid. And then I would hear about it. I've even had to refund part of my commission just to keep from being sued!"

Honestly, Kristen thought her mother was angrier than Mitch was.

"So what's the plan?" Robert Donner asked.

"I—" Mitch began.

"He has no plan," Kristen interrupted. "Except to make Jeremy incriminate himself."

"What good will that do? You'll still look guilty," Patsy said.

"That was *my* point," Kristen told her.

"So *nobody* likes my reasonable doubt defense?" Mitch asked.

"No!" they chorused.

"Although you were saying I was brilliant when Dad got here," Kristen reminded him.

"That's right." Mitch looked more animated. "Because you said that Jeremy and his father would have taken off if they could have. So I figure that something is keeping them here. If I can figure out what, maybe I can use it."

"Well, they are hosting the big Christmas Light Parade kickoff," Mitch's mother said.

Kristen rolled her eyes. Like big-time crooks would risk arrest to give a Christmas party.

"That's it." Mitch beamed at his mother.

"*What*?" Kristen stared at him, and then noticed everyone else nodding and murmuring in agreement.

"A *party*?" Were they all nuts?

"It's not just any party," Patsy said. "It's *the* party."

"It is," Barbara agreed. "The Light Parade is a really big deal now, Kristen. All the politicos are home for the holidays and they make an appearance. Players from the Texans, Rockets and Astros live here, so they're there, too. Even the governor has shown up the past three years."

"The governor of *Texas?*" Kristen could not believe this.

"Sure," Patsy confirmed. "The parade is a feel-good holiday story, so the news media turns out and where there's a news camera, you'll find a politician."

"The Sloanes can't pull out now without attracting all kinds of attention." Carl Zaleski headed for the old-fashioned percolator coffee pot and held it up in a silent question. No one wanted any more coffee. "You have to remember that with an operation this entrenched, they've got some pretty big clients. And those clients aren't exactly Sunday school teachers, if you know what I mean."

Everyone knew what he meant.

He leaned against the coffee bar and actually sipped the nasty stuff out of a thick white mug. Kristen shuddered. "You know, this reminds me of the plot of PALE SHADOWS with Lorna Morelle, Henry Cameron and Rudy Ives."

"That was a good one," Barbara said.

Carl continued, "A secretary is framed by her boss. When she gets out of jail, she frames him, not to the police, but to her boss's mob friends."

"And *they* took care of him. Oh, I like that." Kristen grabbed Mitch's arm. "What do you think?"

"Sounds promising, except for the jail part," he said.

"Oh, you're not going to jail."

Silence in the room.

Kristen glared at everyone. "Well, he's not! Because I like the idea of figuring out who the bad guys are and making them nervous. I mean, we've got all kinds of information. And Mom, you can find out stuff on the real estate end—"

Kristen's mother suddenly stopped pacing. "Kristen Louise Zaleski, is that a belly ring?"

Everyone looked at Kristen's stomach. "Yes."

Typical. They were talking about crime, and framing, and the mob, and keeping Mitch out of jail, and yet her stomach was now center stage.

"I think her belly ring is sexy," Mitch said.

Kristen appreciated his support, but maybe not quite in that way, given that all four of their parents were present and now evaluating the sexiness of her stomach jewelry.

"I suppose it is," Patsy said.

Robert curled his fingers around her hand and leaned toward her. "Why don't you get one?"

They exchanged a look that made Mitch's eyes widen.

Kristen smothered a laugh until she looked up to see that her mother—*her own mother*—had pulled her top out of the waistband of her pants to check out her navel and look questioningly at Kristen's father.

"So," Mitch turned to Kristen with a let's-escape look in his eyes. "I actually have some light installations scheduled for today."

"Without sleep? Since we haven't had any sleep. Because we were here all night. Working," she added for the parents' benefit. But were they listening? No, they were navel gazing.

"I'll be okay. Let me take you home. Hey, you guys didn't wreck my Santa truck, did you?" he asked his parents.

"Santa lives to ho-ho-ho another day," Robert said.

"Mitch." Kristen's mother stopped them. "The Sloanes are not going to get away with this. We'll figure something out."

"Thanks," he replied. "I appreciate you—all of you—believing my side of the story. I'm not sure I believe it myself."

Kristen's father took his leather jacket from where it hung on the back of the desk chair and draped it around her shoulders. "Mitch, just remember that it's easy to lie to an honest man."

"Yeah. Thanks."

That was nice of her dad to say that. Kristen stood on tiptoe and kissed his cheek before she and Mitch left.

"Do you really have to install lights today?" she asked once they were in the car.

Mitch nodded. "Monday I have to start on the Town Square Santa display."

"But Mitch, don't you think you should concentrate on getting out of the mess you're in?"

"I can think while I work." He glanced at her. "I took the job. It's not fair to Sparky to quit right before Christmas."

Kristen could see arguing with him was pointless. "Then maybe I can help you."

"Maybe."

"You sound like you don't think I can string lights or paint or hammer."

"It's not that." He glanced at her. "But you're spending all your time on my problems. What about you?"

This sounded suspiciously like the beginning of a blow-off speech. He wouldn't dare. "What about me?"

"What's your plan? What about your acting? What about your life?"

"My plan is to hang around you because your life is a whole lot more exciting than mine is at the moment."

"Wanna trade?"

Kristen was silent. All those years of busting her butt and everything she owned fit into her luggage, not including the high school leftovers boxed in the attic. And that would be the attic of her parents' home because Kristen didn't have one of her own. But she was rich in experience. Unfortunately she couldn't seem to convert it into a liquid asset.

"You're actually thinking about it!" Mitch turned into Kristen's subdivision.

"Not *seriously*." Except she had been.

"Good. Because there is nothing glamorous or exciting or fun about being double crossed by your best friend, or having your reputation shot to hell, or knowing that the business you poured your life into has been hijacked by criminals."

"No." Kristen swallowed. "No, there isn't." She had nothing, but Mitch had less than nothing.

Actually, that wasn't quite right. He had her.

"Sorry. I'm a little punchy," he said.

"You're entitled."

A few minutes later, they arrived at Kristen's house and Mitch walked her to the door.

Her feet hurt and she wanted a hot bath. "I feel guilty sleeping when I know you can't."

He drew a deep breath. "I couldn't sleep anyway. Too much to think about."

Kristen bumped up against him. "Spend some of that time thinking about me."

He bumped her back. "I already have been. I've been thinking that we wouldn't have connected if everything had gone as planned in our lives."

"So in a weird way, you're grateful to Jeremy."

He gave a short laugh and threw his arm around her shoulders. "No."

She smiled up at him. "I could say I'm insulted,

except I wouldn't have bought the 'grateful to Jeremy' line, either."

"That's not to say I won't take advantage of the situation."

That sounded promising.

They climbed the step to the entryway and Mitch took her hands in his. "Kristen, there is no way I can repay you for what you've done."

"There might be a way," she murmured.

"Seriously, I owe you big time."

Better and better. She swayed toward him.

He squeezed her hands and let them fall. "I'll call you later, okay?"

"Okay."

He leaned down and gave her a quick, dry, unsatisfactory peck on the cheek.

And then he left.

Left.

Left her standing at the front door.

Was it her breath?

Like his would be any better.

Grumbling to herself about clueless men, she unlocked the front door. She was hanging up her dad's jacket in the front closet when there was a knock on the door. "Kristen?"

Mitch.

When she opened the door, he stood there, looking chagrined. "I…forgot."

"Wha—"

That was as far as she got because Mitch stepped forward, cupped her face and kissed her.

Deeply.

Passionately.

Thrillingly.

Or maybe it just seemed that way due to her lack of sleep. In any case, it left her dazzled. Or maybe that was dizziness, again, because of the lack of sleep. But who cared? Certainly not Kristen.

"Good night," he murmured, still holding her face. He gazed into her eyes as he drew his fingers along her jaw and away.

"It's morning," she sighed.

"So it is." And he kissed her again. Deeply, passionately and thrillingly. "Good morning."

"Yes." A dazzled Kristen gripped the doorjamb because of the dizziness. "It is."

Chapter Nine

There was something to be said for mindless jobs, not that anything having to do with electricity and power tools should be mindless. But while one part of Mitch's brain was occupied with stringing lights, the other part, the part that was very good with numbers, was analyzing everything Kristen had showed him and matching it with information stored in his mental files.

His records might have been impounded, but the FBI couldn't take his memory.

And then there was Kristen, who astonishingly, wasn't turned off by a guy who'd demonstrated incredibly bad judgment in picking his friends and was currently, and Mitch hoped temporarily, broke.

Maybe she had a thing for hopeless cases. Maybe he shouldn't overthink this and enjoy the ride while it lasted.

He hoped the ride lasted a long time.

At four o'clock that afternoon, he was finally able to head home to sleep. He called her from his car, partly to keep himself awake and partly to treat himself to her voice.

"Hi. It's your local laundry man. Got anything you need washed?"

"Don't even joke about that," Kristen scolded. "How are you doing?"

"When I close my eyes, I see flashing lights. But I see them when my eyes are open, too."

"You're a nut. Have you had any sleep yet? I slept till noon."

"On my way home now." Mitch smothered a yawn. "What are you doing?"

"I'm at my mom's office going through the files here with her."

He didn't want to ask, but couldn't stop himself. "Did you find anything else?"

"Oh, yeah. Making certain people nervous is going to be a piece of cake."

Mitch didn't ask how it was going to be a piece of cake. He just absorbed the confidence in Kristen's voice, went home, and slept for fourteen hours.

MITCH WAS A BIG BELIEVER in allowing the subconscious mind to work on a problem during sleep. And since it had been mulling over all things Jeremy yesterday, he fully expected to awaken with a plan of action.

Instead, he awoke with Kristen, or rather with thoughts of Kristen. Strong, vivid thoughts. Thoughts of her in her cheerleader-gone-bad outfit. Thoughts of red lips and tight skirts. Thoughts of being surrounded by her hair with her mouth moving over his.

Thoughts of trying to be noble by distancing himself and only lasting halfway down her front walk before coming back to kiss her. Twice. Twice with pretty much everything he had.

Those thoughts.

And his subconscious helpfully analyzed the scene with all four parents and noticed how easily everyone got along even under the circumstances. And how great it felt. And how natural.

His subconscious needed to slow down.

Mitch should get busy. He wanted—needed—to find out when Jeremy had gone bad. Or if he had always been bad. If Mitch was ever going to trust his personal judgment again, he needed to know when it had failed him this time.

He sat at his father's computer and raked his hair back from his face. This early on a Sunday morning it was unlikely that anyone would be working overtime at the office, which was good.

Mitch carefully considered his next move. He hadn't attempted to log into any of his accounts or files mostly because he thought it would look bad. Although Jeremy was no computer genius, there would be a record of activity on the network should anyone be monitoring. Somebody probably was.

But that worked both ways and Mitch knew a few tricks.

He set up a remote identity, logged in using Jeremy's password—the guy had used the same one since college—and had the Sloane and Donner network server dump a copy of all activity from the beginning of November. That was going to take awhile, so he showered and fixed himself a spectacular omelet, if he did say so himself.

Others might say it looked more like stuck-together scrambled eggs with bits of stuff poking through, but it tasted the same.

After he'd washed the dishes, he made a fresh pot of coffee for his parents and went to check on the file transfer.

He passed his parents on the stairs. "We're on our way to church," his mother announced and she didn't look happy about it.

"You ought to come with us," his dad said. "You need the brownie points."

"I know." He needed more than brownie points. "But I'm poking around in our company files while nobody is in the office and I want to keep going. I made coffee."

His father's face lit up. "Real coffee with everything the good Lord intended it to have?"

"Well, yeah. What's the point of decaf?"

"Exactly what I tell your mother."

"Stop complaining, Robert," Patsy said from the bottom of the stairs. "I was going to make regular today, anyway. I want all my wits about me when I have to face the Sloanes in church and pretend I don't know they're ruining my son's life." She stalked into the kitchen.

"Peace on earth, good will toward men," Mitch's dad muttered as he followed her.

When Mitch checked the computer, he found it had finished, so he requested activity files from the previous December through March, which was when Kristen said Anderson Personnel had asked for a credit report.

Mitch suspected it was around that time that Jeremy had Golden Boy "buy" Anderson, thus linking Mitch to the chain of companies and providing a marker to attract the FBI's attention exactly the same way it had attracted Kristen's.

He'd also remembered something else. Five years ago, he and Jeremy had moved GBE from the original offshore account to another bank in another country to practice that type of transferring. He remembered signing the papers. Maybe Jeremy hadn't signed. Maybe that's when he'd taken his name off the account. Mitch wouldn't have known unless he'd deliberately checked since they each had their own access codes.

There'd been a jump in their business around then, too, which was when Mitch had stopped clubbing with Jeremy. They'd drifted into their roles of Mitch as manager of accounts and Jeremy as the one who got the accounts.

It had been crazy busy. They'd moved into a larger space, they'd hired their first full-time employees, and Jeremy was bringing in business faster than Mitch could handle it.

Mitch added a request for the activity logs of five years ago to the queue.

"Bye, Mitch," his mother called from downstairs.

"If we're not back by twelve-thirty, check the news," added his dad.

"Don't worry, I'll control myself."

"Patsy, I'm not worried about you," Mitch heard as the door closed.

He smiled. His parents had been great. Horrified, but great. He didn't envy them facing the Sloanes, but knew it was best to act normally, which meant church on Sunday morning.

Mitch froze. Church on Sunday morning. The Sloanes would be at church.

He called Kristen, hoping she hadn't headed for church, yet, herself.

She answered with, "I was just going to call you. The Sloanes—"

"Are at church right now. I know. I'm going over there."

"What for?"

"I don't know yet. Want to come?"

"Sure."

"I'll pick you up."

"In the *Santa* truck?"

Mitch had given up the rental car weeks ago. "Yes, in the Santa truck. We installed their lights. If anyone bothers to ask, we're doing maintenance. Wear jeans."

Mitch raced over there. Kristen was waiting by the curb. He almost didn't recognize her.

She wore jeans and sneakers and her hair was pulled into a ponytail. If she was wearing any makeup, he couldn't tell.

She yanked open the door and hopped in. "You can put these on." Mitch handed her his extra hoodie and a matching baseball cap.

"Cool." She took off her denim jacket and pulled on the red sweatshirt. Then she stuck her ponytail through the back of the cap and fastened the seatbelt. "How do I look?"

"Like you're about twelve."

"Kinky."

Mitch squealed away from the curb. "We did kinky Friday night. You look very girl-next-door."

"Oh, good. I was going for fresh-scrubbed high school girl."

"*You* didn't look like that in high school."

"Of course not. I was popular. Anyway, I'm not pretending to be me." She eyed him. "You should wear a cap, too."

"I don't do caps."

"You don't want to be recognized."

"Trust me. No one is going to pay any attention to us in that neighborhood."

"What if Mr. and Mrs. Sloane decided to skip church today?"

She had a point. "There's another cap in the glove compartment."

Kristen dug it out and wrinkled her nose.

"I gave you the clean one," Mitch said.

"I appreciate it." She ruffled his hair.

"Hey, watch it. I'm driving. What are you doing?"

"Experimenting. Hold still."

Basically, she messed his hair up and set the cap way back on his head. "There. Your eyes look bigger."

He glanced at his reflection in the rearview. "Caps are not worn this way. I look like a dork." He resettled it on his forehead, but now hair stuck out in front of his eyes. "Kristen."

"Okay." She fingercombed his hair back and carefully positioned the cap on his head.

Mitch pulled the bill down. "Covers more of my face this way."

"I give up." But she sounded only mildly annoyed. "So. What are we looking for?"

"I have no idea. I just thought I'd take the opportunity to look around. We've only got about forty-five minutes."

"Have you been to their house before?"

Mitch shook his head. "Have you?"

"No. I would have thought you might have visited Jeremy there."

"Jeremy and I didn't really know each other until college and his folks only moved into that place about five years ago."

"No doubt when the construction company really started to take off," Kristen said dryly.

"No doubt." The time period beginning five years ago was cropping up more and more. Five years. *Five.*

He couldn't think about it.

He zoomed through Sugar Land on Highway 6 at a speed that would normally have gotten him face time with the local police and he doubted he could declare a lighting emergency. But the good folks of Sugar Land were all in church this holiday season and there weren't that many bad folks. Which was why the Sloanes were so successful. No one would suspect a generous contributor to community causes. No one would *want* to suspect a generous contributor to community causes.

"The Sloane house is a huge showplace," Kristen said. "Right on the golf course and next to a lake. Mom says they had to get the land rezoned so they could keep people from building in front of them and blocking their view."

"Must be nice."

"Now, now. Don't be bitter."

"Why not?"

"You'll get wrinkles."

Mitch laughed. He couldn't help it. "I haven't had time to get bitter."

"Well, don't bother." The tone of Kristen's voice changed and she gazed out the window as they passed houses that became more upscale and the exterior Christmas decorations more elaborate. "Bitterness is a backward emotion. You're stuck in the past instead of living in the present and looking to the future."

"People can be bitter in the present."

Kristen shook her head. "People can be dissatisfied in the present."

"Are you talking about yourself?"

"Yes and no. I'm in transition, I guess. I need to set new goals, but I'm not sure what they should be."

Yes. Let's discuss her problems for a change. Before he could respond, she pointed to a small, cutesy country-style decorated wooden sign by a private road.

"I think this is it. 'Chuck's Stake.' Very funny. It must have been a gift."

Mitch turned onto the narrow asphalt drive. "I'm going to park around by the garage."

"Okay. And then what?" she asked, very reasonably.

"I'll give you a voltmeter and you can pretend to take readings. Tell anyone who asks that there were complaints of flickering lights and we're checking for broken wires and shorts. If they give you any trouble, start throwing around the words 'fire hazard' and 'liability release.'"

"Ooo. Liability release. That's a good one."

"Thanks. I don't know if The Electric Santa has such a thing. I just made it up."

"Well, what if they want to sign one?"

Did he have to think of everything? "I don't know... tell them you don't have a copy with you because nobody has ever been stupid enough to want to sign one!"

"You're very good at this," Kristen said. "I'm impressed. If things don't go well for you, you might consider working for my dad."

Mitch parked the car. "If things don't go well for me, I'll have a felony conviction."

"Yeah. Bummer."

"Bummer?" He stared at her. "That's all you can say?"

"Shh. I'm getting into character. It's stupid to argue about your possible future hypothetical felony conviction. Now, I've got my story. I've got my character—what's my mission?"

Mitch had really hoped something would occur to him by now. They both stared at the house—mansion—Southern plantation—whatever. There was a pool. A guesthouse. A barbecue pit big enough to roast a steer. There was a garage complex and mechanic's bay. When Mitch looked to one side, he saw a boat house with a dock and a sleek little cruiser in the slip. On the other side, the yard yielded to the golf course. Two golf carts were parked at the end of the private cart path that merged into the course paths.

Mitch tried not to think about how much dirty money had paid for this or where it had been to get dirty.

"I wonder what kind of crime bought this place," Kristen said.

"I was trying not to think about it."

"You know, after we take the Sloanes down, the government will confiscate this property and sell it at an auction. Wouldn't it be cool to buy it? The ultimate revenge."

"Buy it with what?"

She blinked at him. "With Jeremy's half of the business, which you will own because you very cleverly wrote a fraud clause into your partnership agreement."

"Nice fantasy."

"Oh." They stared at the house. "I should have known you were the handshake type."

"It might surprise you to know that it was Jeremy who didn't need more than a handshake. Bringing in lawyers after that seemed like a lack of good faith."

"I'm not surprised. But Jeremy will be." She smiled at him. "This is Texas, after all. A handshake has serious clout. You'll be better off."

"Especially if I prove I shook hands with a snake."

"Uh—"

"Just go with it." They were wasting time. "Okay. This is where the kickoff party will be, right?"

"Yes."

"So we'll just poke around for now. Let's look for power outlets at the edge of the house and pretend to trace the light strings. Look in the windows and maybe we'll get lucky and see something."

"Like a sign that says 'money-laundering operation world headquarters'?"

"Yeah, like that," Mitch said.

Kristen made a face and got out of the car. "In your dreams."

Mitch slammed the door. "You have yours and I'll have mine."

Kristen took the meter he handed her and jogged up to the house. "I should have an iPOD," he thought he heard her say.

He stared at the house and wondered if any staff were on the premises. If he could get inside, then...then what? Sneak into the office and download the contents of the computer? Right. Except records of their laundering had to be kept somewhere. Would Chuck Sloane keep it on his home computer? Office computer? Jeremy's computer? No computer at all?

Kristen came jogging back. "There are lights outlining the windows. Why don't you get the ladder out of the truck?" She bounced from side to side.

"What are you doing?"

"Teenagers have lots of energy."

He liked the way her ponytail flipped around. "You're short."

"Five-five is not short. Five-five is average. I was wearing heels before."

"Oh." He continued to watch her. The bouncing was quite nice.

"Mitch?"

"Huh?"

"I am only pretending to be a teenager, therefore I do not have a teenager's energy. Please get the ladder!"

They carried the ladder to the front of the house. Mitch climbed it to check out the upper windows and Kristen prowled around beneath him and spied into the lower ones.

"See if it looks as though they're getting ready to

leave. Maybe packing boxes or something," Mitch called down to her.

"They can't really pull up chuck stakes now—ha ha. Get it?"

"Yeees."

"Well, they can't pack before the party. It would look funny and people would ask questions."

"I suppose you're right." Mitch's frustration mounted. The problem with living life on the straight and narrow was that he had no experience with the crooked and wide. "See if you can find the office."

They'd moved around to the side of the house before Kristen located the ground floor office. Mitch had climbed down the ladder and was looking inside when they heard the purr of a car engine coming from the golf course side.

"They can't be back already!" Kristen turned a panicked face toward him.

"Worse." Mitch stared at the approaching car. The lapis metallic blue car. "That's a Porsche 911 Carrera S Cabriolet. Jeremy's car." He drew a long, fortifying breath. "I wonder what kind of damage a plastic Santa can do to a Porsche 911 Carrera S Cabriolet."

"It depends on whether it's attached to a truck at the time." Kristen clamped both hands around his arm. "Get back up on the ladder," she ordered. "Keep your face turned away and make some noise with the staple gun. I'll talk to him."

"Don't talk to him!" Mitch climbed the ladder. "Ignore him. You're checking for wiring problems. You'll be invisible to him."

She put one hand on her hip. "Oh, honey, I am *never* invisible to men."

"You're supposed to be in *high school!*"

"I wasn't invisible then, either."

This was not going to go well.

Jeremy drove the car toward the garage with an impressive waste of power. He screeched to a pinpoint stop. Gravel pinged Mitch's ladder.

What was Jeremy doing here now? It was over a week until Christmas—who was running the company? Other than tax-time, this was their busiest time of the year. Who was looking after their clients? Did they *have* any clients left? Real ones?

Mitch had a horrible thought. Had they ever had real clients?

The thought made him queasy, which wasn't good since he was on a ladder.

A door slammed. In the reflection on the window glass, Mitch watched Jeremy's progress. He withdrew an overnighter, hanging bag and a duffel.

He was obviously home for Christmas.

"Hey, there." It was the friendly opener Jeremy used with women. And he was using it on Kristen.

Had he recognized her? Mitch let loose with a couple of staples.

"Hey," she responded. "Nice car."

No! Hadn't he told her not to talk to Jeremy?

"Thanks. I haven't had it long. It was my twenty-fifth birthday present to myself."

Liar. And shaving years off his age?

"Sweet." Kristen moved closer.

Jeremy dumped his luggage off to the side. "Want to go for a ride?"

Mitch abused the windowsill with a flurry of staples.

"Can't. I'm working." She bounced a little.

No bouncing.

Jeremy leaned against his car in "the pose." Mitch had taken pictures of him in "the pose." There was a framed one in Jeremy's office.

"So what are you working on?"

"Oh—" she flung an arm toward the house "—some of the lights are messin' up so we're fixing them."

Jeremy glanced up at Mitch, who pretended to be checking bulbs. If there had been a real problem, it would have been far more cost effective to replace the string and be done with it. He hoped Jeremy didn't think of that.

"What are you doing *after* you fix the lights?"

"Writing a paper." Kristen's unenthusiastic voice brought back memories.

"College?"

"No, silly." She giggled. "High school. I'm a senior."

She should have gone with college, Mitch grumbled to himself. He let loose with another barrage of staples. He could only stay up here so long. It was just a string of icicle Christmas lights. He looked at the line of staples. When the lights came down, they'd probably bring the windowsill with them.

In the sudden silence, he caught the last of what Kristen was saying.

"...cheerleader."

What? *What*?

"Ready? O-*kay!*" She positioned herself, hands on hips, feet together. "We're the sweetest, you're so sour..."

She was doing a cheer. A cheer. For Jeremy. Mitch risked looking down.

"...you've got nothing, we've got power!"

Now she was jumping up and down squealing, "Yea, Sugar Land!"

Jeremy was lapping it up.

And Mitch? Mitch was flashing back to Friday night's outfit. Someday...

But back to Jeremy, who did not know about Friday night's outfit and should not be lapping up anything of high school age.

"Good ole Sugar Land," Jeremy was saying. "Hey, I don't know your name. I'm Jeremy."

Mitch tried to drown out Kristen with the staple gun, but the thing quit working.

"Krissie."

Krissie was too close to Kristen. She was going to give him heart failure.

"Well, Krissie, I'm staying with my parents this week. There's supposed to be some party here."

No. He wouldn't. Actually, Jeremy would. But Kristen—no. No, she wouldn't dare. Mitch smacked the staple gun against the side of the house. Why wouldn't the stupid thing work?

"Oh, yeah! It's for the Light Parade volunteers. Everybody will be here."

"Including you?" Jeremy's voice was low and sexy. Not sexy to Mitch, but no doubt appealing to a high school girl who didn't know any better.

"Well, duh!" chirped Kristen.

Mitch snickered under his breath.

"Maybe I can take you for a ride then," Jeremy said. "We can see all the lights. You can fill me in on what's happening at Sugar Land High these days."

Incredible. The man was hitting on a high school girl.

"I can't." She sounded convincingly disappointed. "I'll be working the parade and there's no way Mom and Dad will let me go out that late."

Good girl.

She looked down and fiddled with the voltmeter. "I've got finals this week, but we could get together after the party." She bit her lip and gazed at him from beneath her cap.

Bad girl.

Mitch really hoped she saw the smug I've-got-you-and-I-know-it expression on Jeremy's face before he inhaled and unfolded his arms. "The 'rents and I are going skiing right after the party." Bending down, he retrieved his luggage. "Unless you're up for a study break, it looks like you'll miss out."

Skiing? During the last trading days of the year? No. No no *no*.

"I *love* to ski," gushed Kristen.

What was she doing, angling for an invitation?

"Where are you going?"

"Engleberg." He started toward the house. "It's in Switzerland."

Land of the anonymous bank accounts.

"Wow. How long are you gonna be there?"

"As long as the skiing is good."

"You're lucky."

Jeremy unlocked the door. "Luck is nothing more than taking advantage of an opportunity."

Was that what Mitch was? An opportunity? He squeezed the staple gun so tightly his hand went numb.

"Well…if you feel like taking advantage of an opportunity, I might need a ride home from school." Kristen tilted her head and toyed with the meter she held.

Jeremy flashed his perfectly bleached and bonded teeth. "You know what my car looks like." And he went into the house.

Chapter Ten

The door had barely closed before Mitch climbed down the ladder and folded it. "Let's go, Lolita." He took off toward the truck.

"Shouldn't we—"

Mitch stopped walking and glared at her before continuing toward the truck. She could follow or not. If she needed a ride, *Jeremy* could give her one.

"Mitch."

He didn't trust himself to answer. He wanted to toss the metal ladder into the truck bed, but, because he was Mitch the thoughtful, Mitch the good guy, Mitch the dependable, he carefully loaded the ladder so it wouldn't scratch the paint.

But he slammed the tailgate.

He stalked around to the driver's side and got in.

Kristen was already inside, seatbelt fastened. "Let's hope Jeremy isn't watching your little tantrum."

Mitch started the truck and shifted gears as though he'd never driven a stick before. "He'll just think I'm jealous."

Kristen mulled that over. "Are you jealous?"

"*No!*"

"Because you don't need to be."

"I am not jealous."

"You're *something*, and you can't be mad at me because *I* rocked." She counted off on her fingers. "We now know he and his parents are leaving the country, and I can show up at the party—"

"You were going anyway."

"*And* I set it up so I can see him before then in case you need a distraction."

"I don't need that kind of distraction. What were you thinking?" They'd made it down the back drive to the "Chuck's Stake" sign without Mitch running into anything and he'd really, *really* wanted to clip the bumper of a certain metallic lapis blue Porsche 911 Carrera S Cabriolet.

"I was thinking that we were there to get information. I was thinking that we weren't doing so well until Jeremy drove up."

"He could have recognized you."

"Not a chance."

How could she be so calmly certain when he still couldn't breathe normally? "Kristen…your face was on a *billboard* in Sugar Land when you were Miss Sweetest."

"I was wearing a crown and make up." She slid him a glance that he saw out of the corner of his eye as he turned onto the main road. "*You* didn't recognize me that first day at Noir Blanc."

True.

"*You* were in more danger of being recognized. But Jeremy saw what he wanted to see. He wanted to impress a high school girl."

"That's sick."

Kristen drew her knees up and wrapped her arms around them. It was a youthful gesture and she *looked* like a high school girl.

"You shouldn't have talked to him for so long."

"Mitch, you weren't the only one I checked out. I know Jeremy's type. I met enough of them in Hollywood. He's compensating."

"For *what*?" From Mitch's point of view, Jeremy had it all.

"For being overlooked. Not taken seriously. Dismissed. For not being admired or popular. I remembered a couple of things about him from school and I looked him up in my sophomore yearbook—when you guys were seniors. I think he's one of those people who desperately wants to be popular, so he lets people use him in hopes that they'll like him and then he'll be popular, too. Only it never works out that way. They'll take what he gives, but they'll never give back."

Mitch considered that while he negotiated the increasingly heavy traffic. "High school was a long time ago."

"It shapes us."

"Then Jeremy was warped," Mitch grumbled.

"Here's the thing. Jeremy believes that he's better than everyone else and he wants it acknowledged."

Maybe Mitch had known that about Jeremy, but it hadn't bothered him. An arrogant self-confidence and a flashy personality had been good for business. Mitch hadn't recognized that it had been the wrong business.

Kristen continued. "So when he drove up in his hot little car, I acted impressed."

"You were supposed to ignore him."

"And lose the opportunity to learn something?"

She was right. However, "Exactly where did your little sweet and sour dance fit in?"

"Didja like that?" She grinned widely.

"I would have liked it more if you'd been wearing Friday's outfit."

She reached out and finger-walked down his thigh. "That can be arranged."

Mitch gripped the steering wheel as a wave of unexpected lust gripped him.

"I've got some really great pompoms," she added.

"Which you must never, ever show to Jeremy." The woman was going to drive him crazy.

Judging by her smug grin, she knew it, too. "That's the point. I became the cute, flirty cheerleader. The kind of girl who wouldn't have noticed him in high school. But I sure noticed him now."

"Just like every other woman," Mitch said in disgust. He honestly hadn't meant to say that out loud.

"Mitch!" She poked him. "Oh, come on."

"Kristen, I know you pegged his type, but people—especially women people—like that type. When we'd go out, they were all over him."

"That's because they knew he'd buy them drinks!" Her mouth was open in astonishment. "And he did, didn't he?"

Mitch nodded.

"I bet he put it on his expense account, too."

Mitch nodded again. He'd argued with Jeremy about it. Jeremy had told him to lighten up. Mitch had told him their company couldn't afford it if they both lightened up. Jeremy had quoted the old "You have to spend money to make money" adage and that no one would hire them to manage their money if it looked as though they weren't rich themselves. Instead of being fiscally responsible, Mitch was actually hurting the company. So Mitch had backed off.

And when the business poured in, he couldn't argue with what worked.

It wasn't that Mitch was *jealous* of Jeremy's appeal, but he was curious. "How did they know he'd buy them drinks?"

"The hotties?"

Mitch shifted in the seat. "It depends on your definition of hot."

"Me, Friday night. I was smokin'."

Letting out a long breath, he said quietly, "You're always smokin'." He glanced at her. "Always."

She gave him a wide smile. "Mitch, you sweetie."

Mitch did not want to be a sweetie. Not in this context. "Just pat me on the head and get it over with."

Kristen promptly thwapped him on the head.

He ducked. "Hey! I was speaking metaphorically."

"You were speaking stupidly. Jeremy is easy to size up as a man who needs arm candy to feel important. He buys them drinks so they'll stick around. Otherwise, they wouldn't."

They were nearly back to Kristen's house. "There's got to be more to it than that," Mitch said.

"Why?"

"Because it's so…"

"Shallow?"

"Pathetic. They're using him."

"He's using them! He doesn't care about anything

but the way they look and the hotter the better. He wants every man in that room to envy him."

"I don't envy him."

"Because you wouldn't have to bribe a hottie to stick with you. You *are* the bribe. And don't think Jeremy isn't aware of that."

He smiled slightly. "Yes, but are *women* aware of that?"

"Okay, well I did make you buy me a margarita," she admitted with a laugh. "One. But look at all the mileage you've gotten out of it."

In spite of himself, Mitch's smile widened. "I always had a knack for picking good investments."

"Listen." Kristen let go of her knees and swiveled to face him. "Jeremy may look great with his expensive haircut, his buffed nails, his bronze skin and his bleached teeth."

"Not that you noticed."

She ignored him. "He can have the car and the cash and the expensive watch and the designer clothes while you've got nothing—"

"Thanks for reminding me."

"And you know what eats at him? He knows you're still more of a man than he could ever be."

Mitch pulled next to the curb in front of Kristen's house and killed the engine. "You really are a cheerleader."

"The words you're looking for are 'thank you, Kristen.'"

Instead of thanking her, Mitch reached out and tugged on her ponytail until she'd leaned within range. And then he kissed her.

It was just your basic you're-an-incredible-woman-and-I-don't-deserve-you kiss, but it was still a pretty good one. It was rich and layered and packed an emotional wallop that Jeremy would never experience with his shallow, anonymous hotties.

As Mitch pulled back and gazed into Kristen's eyes, he pitied Jeremy.

"Mmm. You're welcome," she whispered.

He released her ponytail and leaned against the truck's door.

She held his gaze for just a second before intently studying her thumbnail. "You're staring at me."

"I like looking at you."

Every time he saw her, she looked like a different woman. At first, he'd noticed her voice and her lips. Then she was all eyes. Today, he could see the bare canvas—the face he'd see on the pillow next to his when he woke up in the mornings. Simple, quiet beauty.

Jeremy could keep his dazzle and flash.

He smiled.

"What?" she asked.

"Were you ever arm candy?"

Kristen dropped her head back and groaned. "Of course! There are a lot of men who need their egos stroked. That's all I was doing with Jeremy."

"He wanted a lot more than being stroked," Mitch told her darkly.

"No, he'd insist on doing the stroking." Kristen pulled the baseball cap off and freed her ponytail. "And he'd want to be told he was the best ever, which he wouldn't be because with that kind of guy, it's all about the technique. And it's never great when it's all about the technique."

Mitch made a mental note.

"But those guys never get that because they're emotional cripples. And you realize they'll never get it and that it isn't about you, it's about them, and so you want the whole thing over with."

"I can see that." They were veering into a territory Mitch didn't really want to explore with her.

Kristen looked around for her jacket and grabbed it from behind the seats. "Only they're not going to stop because they're the best, and by golly, nothing less than your screaming gratitude will satisfy them. And so you fake it."

"You fake, er, gratitude?"

"Sometimes you have to." She was so nonchalant about it.

"Oh." He swallowed. "Does that happen…a lot?"

His voice must have given him away because she laughed as she pulled her arms out of the sleeves of the sweatshirt. "Don't worry. I won't have to fake it with you."

Hello? Mitch sat up.

Kristen pulled the sweatshirt over her head and then seemed to realize what she'd said. Her cheeks turned pink as she folded the shirt and handed it to him.

Mitch caught her eye and grinned. "Good to know."

A COUPLE OF DAYS LATER, Kristen picked her way across the Town Center grass to where Mitch and The Electric Santa team were building a King Kong–sized Santa Claus who would be overseeing his workshop, represented by the floats in the light parade. The massive structure would be the center of the display. It was fixed in position and after the parade, the floats would park around it, and complete the scene.

She heard someone call her name and waved to Mitch's mom, who, along with Nora Beckman, was assigning display spaces to the parade floats.

All around them, volunteers roped off part of the City Hall parking lot and marked the grassy area for the float display. Vendors were starting to set up their booths and electricians were running extra power cables and lights. City workers had posted temporary directional signs and erected barriers along the parade route. Traffic had already been rerouted to accommodate all the additional visitors and keep it moving around the display site without blocking the regular flow.

This thing was out of control, Kristen thought. When she'd reigned as Miss Sweetest, the parade had consisted of her float, all sugary white, a few high school bands and their drill teams, bagpipers, the local vintage auto club, a church handbell choir in Dickensian costumes, the sheriff's mounted patrol, some caroling groups, a fire truck, maybe another couple of floats sponsored by whatever business wanted the advertising, and bringing up the rear, Santa Claus, who threw candy to the crowd.

Everyone had been thrilled.

Now, parking near the area was a nightmare. Everybody in Sugar Land was either working on the parade or Christmas shopping at the nearby mall.

At Noir Blanc, business had slowed, which was

good because Kristen's mother and her super secret cadre of real estate colleagues were going after Sloane Property Development and Construction with everything they had, which was a lot once they started matching names with information Mitch had given them.

Several of those names had local connections. Kristen wondered if Mitch knew that his father was playing detective. Robert Donner had been an oil company salesman and used his talents to line up sponsors for the annual parade. Now, he was calling on their suspects under the guise of asking for last-minute donations. While he was at it, he threw in a few seemingly casual remarks praising the Sloanes for going ahead with the party, even though they were leaving the country shortly afterward. This information visibly unnerved some of the people. Those names made the hot list.

Kristen found Mitch standing on top of a four-foot-tall plywood platform that would conceal the controls and power source for the Santa Claus.

Kristen shaded her eyes and squinted up at the Santa's support structure. "You're going to frighten small children with that thing."

"Hey." Mitch shoved his safety glasses to the top of his head and grinned down at her. "And you haven't seen the arms move yet."

It was a warm, muggy day, typical in a month of flip-flopping weather when cool fronts blowing in from the north battled with the moist air over the Gulf of Mexico. Today was not a day for black wool, which was what Kristen wore.

Mitch had abandoned his sweatshirt and was wearing just a thin white tee shirt with his jeans.

If he walked into a bar right now and looked at the women the way he was looking at her, she'd guarantee they'd be all over him. And *they'd* be buying the drinks.

"Ready for a lunch break?" Kristen held up a cooler.

"You betcha." He unbuckled his tool belt, an action that caused a few flutters in Kristen's middle, and set it and his safety glasses next to the edge. Then he squatted and jumped down, landing beside her.

She openly gave him the once over. "You're looking very manly, today."

"And you're looking very womanly, as always." His eyes crinkled.

Kristen hadn't seen his eyes crinkle since before he learned about Jeremy. He did a good crinkle. "You're in a good mood."

Mitch spread a packing quilt over the edge of the plywood. "I ought to be. A hot babe just brought me lunch."

"That's good-lookin' dame to you." Kristen appreciated the flattery, but there was something else going on. She'd let him bring it up.

Patting the quilt, he said, "This should prevent another stocking disaster like we had yesterday."

When she'd joined him on the platform for lunch, the rough wood edges had snagged and shredded her fragile vintage stockings.

"We don't want them to run since they're expensive, genuine vintage, seamed stockings that you order off the Internet," he quoted.

She laughed. "I can't believe you remembered that."

He took the cooler from her. "You may have mentioned it once or twice."

"Sorry."

"Not a problem. I've developed a fondness for the genuine vintage, black-seamed stockings that you order off the Internet."

"In England, they've kept a few of the old machines that manufactured old-style stockings going. Can you believe it?"

Mitch looked her in the eyes. "Yes."

Hmm. So Mitch might be a lingerie man. Not that she was likely to know for certain at the rate things were going. Which was slow. Kisses and meaningful intense looks were all very well and good, but they weren't leading to anything more.

Even her revealing slip on Sunday hadn't moved things along. She really hoped he wasn't waiting for the mess with Jeremy to be cleared up, but was very much afraid he was.

While she wasn't against a woman making the first move—or even the second and third move—at some point, the man was going to have to make a move back. Or rather, forward, because even the most understanding woman needed positive reinforcement. Technically, Mitch's good night/good morning kisses could be considered positive reinforcement, but Kristen honestly could do with a little more enthusiasm.

"Hang on." Placing his hands around her waist, Mitch hoisted her onto the platform.

Kristen straightened her skirt. "I tell you, when women wore these outfits, they couldn't move around much."

Mitch hopped up beside her. "Made them easier to catch."

Kristen refrained from pointing out that she wasn't running and he wasn't chasing. Instead, she took the lid off the cooler.

Mitch rubbed his hands together. "Thanks, honey. What have we got today? A ham sandwich and potato salad? Some of your dee-lishus fried chicken and chocolate cake?"

She handed him a black-bottomed plastic clam shell container. "California roll with wakame seaweed and sesame salad and an order of edamame."

"That was my next guess." He cast a wary eye at the container.

"Here are your chopsticks. There's a bottle of green tea in the cooler."

Mitch looked at the chopsticks and then at Kristen.

"What? Don't you know how to use them?"

"Sure, but edamame and chopsticks? After I spent the morning wielding a hammer and other manly tools?"

"There's a packet with a napkin and fork taped to the bottom of the plate."

"Now we're talking." Mitch ripped open the plastic with his teeth. Removing the fork, he made a show of digging it into the pile of edamame.

Kristen watched him and then used her fingers to pick up the beans. "It's like a snack food." She popped a couple into her mouth.

"You just didn't want to use chopsticks, either."

Kristen smiled. "I saw your mom over there. How's Nora Beckman working out for her?"

Mitch looked over at his mother. "Great. Mom's

using her as the kickoff party liaison to avoid dealing with the Sloanes."

"That's probably a good thing." Between Mitch's problems and overseeing the entire Christmas Light Parade and everything that went with it, Kristen was surprised Patsy Donner hadn't cracked. "Although I don't know about Nora Beckman being the only thing between your mother and the Sloanes."

"Mrs. Beckman has been really up front about her drinking problem and wants to keep busy."

"After seeing this place, I don't think that'll be too hard." Kristen tangled the strands of seaweed with her chopsticks. They slithered off.

"Snack food?" Mitch asked.

"Fork food." She gave in and unpeeled her condiment pack. "Did Mrs. Beckman tell you about her twin brother?"

"That they were born on Christmas and he and his family were killed coming to visit her? Yeah."

"Mr. Beckman says she blames herself."

Mitch tore open a packet of soy sauce. "Her brother was piloting his own plane, right?"

Kristen nodded. "They'd never missed spending the day together."

Mitch soaked his sushi in the dark liquid. "I hate hearing stuff like this."

"I know." Kristen picked at her salad, but didn't eat any. "Anyway, the weather delayed flights and naturally, Mrs. Beckman was disappointed."

"It was still his decision to fly." Mitch spread an alarming amount of wasabi on his sushi.

"But she's convinced that if she hadn't made such a

big deal about it when her brother called that he *wouldn't* have decided to fly and they'd all still be alive."

Mitch had started shaking his head before Kristen finished. "He had his wife and kids with him. If he took off in that plane, it was because he thought it was safe to fly. No man would risk his family just to show up for Christmas a few hours earlier."

Just understanding that showed that Mitch was good father material, Kristen thought, knowing she was getting *way* ahead of herself, but not particularly minding.

"Any more soy sauce?" he asked.

"You can have the rest of mine." She gave it to him and he promptly added to the lake his sushi was already swimming in. "You know wasabi is super hot, right?"

"It's the only manly food in this lunch," he grumbled.

"Well, pardon me for trying to keep you healthy and alert while you use your manly power tools this afternoon." Miffed, Kristen stabbed at her salad.

"Aww. You brought me seaweed because you care." He gave her a sappy grin.

"It looks like somebody is going to be getting his own lunch the rest of the week."

"And he'll be getting it over there." Mitch was looking at something behind her.

Kristen turned around and saw Patsy talking with one of the booth workers. Nora was helping another woman hang up their sign. "Sausage on a Stick. Mitch!"

"Oh, that's nothing. Mom is all excited because they're debuting a new food here. Batter-fried fruitcake."

"Don't even joke about that."

"I swear I'm not." He held up his hand, palm outward. "They dunk a slice of fruitcake in funnel cake batter and deep fry it."

"*Why?*"

"There's not much that can't be improved by a few minutes in a deep fat fryer."

Kristen leveled a look at him. "You're going to try some, aren't you?"

Mitch grinned. "Hell, yeah."

Sagging, she closed her eyes. "I give up."

"Hey, just because somebody's skirt is getting tight is no reason to make all of us suffer."

Kristen's eyes popped open in horror. "It's supposed to be tight!" She looked down at herself. That was fabric pooching over her lap and not her stomach, right? Right? Cautiously, she extended her index finger and pressed, relieved when the extra poof deflated. Not disappeared, she had to admit, but at least it moved.

She looked up to find Mitch regarding her. His lips barely curved upward in that quiet way he had that made him look *very* attractive, as though he'd decided to ravish her, knew she wanted to be ravished and that it was only a matter of picking his moment.

Which was exactly the case. Furthermore, she'd tossed any number of moments his way and he hadn't caught any of them.

She was about to lob another but stopped when she saw the expression in his eyes. Fond amusement, that's what it was. Fond. Amusement.

Okay, so this wasn't the place for barely restrained lust, but banked desire would have worked. Would have worked big time, thank you very much.

She sat up straight and automatically sucked in her

stomach and then, angry with herself, let it out again. "I hadn't realized that you—"

"Kristen!" Mitch laughed. "You look—"

"Stop." She glared at him. "Think very carefully about what you say next. Because if you're going to say I look 'fine,' you should be aware that I consider *fine* several levels beneath me."

"Okay." He gazed his lunch. "Let's say you look—"

"It better not be 'healthy.' Healthy is another word for big, and that's just another way of saying fat."

"But women are supposed to have—"

"If you are about to say 'curves,' don't. 'Curves' is code for big hips, meaning fat."

Visibly exasperated, he asked, "Then what's *fat* the word for?"

"You think I'm *faaaat*?" Kristen wailed.

"I think I'm going to eat my lunch." Mitch ate two dripping pieces of sushi as Kristen sat there.

He squinted off into the distance. "You know, even the Japanese like to deep fry stuff in batter. They call it *tempura*."

"Okay, okay." She waited. "You aren't going to tell me what you were going to say, are you?"

"Nope." Mitch picked up another piece of California roll. "My mother is on her way over here. Try to look like you're enjoying yourself or she'll think something horrible has happened."

"I *am* enjoying myself."

He smiled down at her. "So am I."

That was better. The fondness had definitely warmed to affection. And if she was not mistaken, it was simmering its way to attraction.

Mollified, Kristen finally captured the slippery strands of her salad.

"Hi, you two," Patsy greeted them. "Nora and I are going to have lunch at the mall and pick up the sponsor booklets from the printer."

Nora Beckman was gazing up at the Santa Claus. "Wow. And I thought last year's was big."

Patsy cast an assessing glance at the float. "Are you sure this will be done in time, Mitch?"

"Are you asking as my mother or as the parade's supreme commander?"

Concern crossed her face. "Are the answers different?"

"No, I just wondered whether or not to salute."

"Don't get snippy with me, Mitchell Donner."

Kristen snickered.

"You see what I put up with?" Patsy said to Nora, who was smiling.

"Yes, Mother, the float will be finished in time," Mitch assured her.

"Good. We've hired extra security this year, but we think the crowds are going to be even bigger than projected. You should talk to Sparky about keeping a watch on this."

"We've got it covered. We're setting up video surveillance so that whoever is inside here working the controls can monitor outside activity. And we're also going to have two ways in and out." Mitch pointed to a four-foot opening in the side of the platform. "That's going to be a doll house, but the door will really work. There will also be a utility opening where the power cords come in."

Patsy nodded and made a note in her binder. "I hate

that we have to think about the possibility of vandalism, but the parade draws so many outsiders." Her lips tightened. "Though we know that not everyone living in Sugar Land can be trusted, either."

Mitch and Kristen exchanged looks.

"Well, we're off." She glanced at their food. "That looks yummy. What do you think, Nora? Should we go for Japanese or stick with the Texas burger, home fries and eggnog shakes?"

Mitch whimpered and Kristen nudged him with her elbow.

"We ought to take advantage of those eggnog shakes while we can," Nora was saying as they walked off. "They're seasonal, you know."

Mitch stared after them.

Kristen sighed. "If you want an eggnog shake, I will go get you one."

"I do, but I wasn't thinking about that. Mrs. Beckman should stop blaming herself."

"People are always blaming themselves for stuff that isn't their fault," Kristen said.

"I hope you're not including me." Mitch poked at his seaweed salad.

"Of course, I'm including you!" She leaned over to see that he was basically moving the salad around in its compartment. "Eat that. It's good for you."

Mitch stabbed a forkful of salad and held it up. "Why is it that slimy green stuff is always good for you and crisp brown stuff isn't?"

"Bran," Kristen retorted. "Crisp and brown."

"Bran is not crisp. Bran is chewy." But he ate his salad.

"Speaking of things not your fault, have you heard

from Jeremy?" She'd hesitated to ask, but the party was in three days and Jeremy had said he was leaving after that.

Mitch shook his head and withdrew his phone. "But I expect to. Let me check my e-mail." He stared at the tiny screen. "Nothing yet. Maybe he'll call."

"Why? What have you done?"

"What makes you think—okay. I logged into our office files using Jeremy's password when I found out mine no longer worked."

"Why would you think your password would work? They kicked you out."

"Actually, they didn't. I left because Jeremy thought it would look better. It was near Thanksgiving, so I went home. Which got me to thinking."

This looked like it was going to be a long story. "Before you think—do you want your pickled ginger?"

"Take it."

"Thanks." Kristen speared it with her fork. "Okay, what were you thinking?"

"It's been weeks. Why haven't I been arrested? They tipped their hand by impounding all my stuff." Mitch reached into the cooler and withdrew the bottles of tea, twisted off the caps and handed her one. "They haven't even brought me in for questioning or whatever."

"My dad thinks it's because they didn't find what they expected to."

"I've got a theory." Mitch took a long swallow of tea.

All that soy sauce had made him thirsty, Kristen thought.

"Jeremy did a heavy-handed thorough job of setting me up. It was too easy. These investigators have seen a lot of cases and, since I was oblivious, I wasn't fitting the pattern. I went home to visit my folks. I didn't contact my shifty clients, and anytime I talked with Jeremy, I'd ask if he had any idea of what was happening. So, they find this trail in my records. But they don't find any in my e-mail or any of my accounts, or anywhere in my stuff."

Kristen had been eating her sushi as he talked. It wouldn't hurt to cut back. "But you wouldn't have been stupid enough to use your regular records and e-mail. You'd set up hidden ones." She set one of her California roll pieces into Mitch's soy sauce lake.

"Exactly. So why would I be stupid enough to leave all the financial records on my office computer?" He ate her sushi piece.

"You wouldn't." She drank some of her tea and pretended not to notice when Mitch stole the last of her sushi. "And somebody realized that. They haven't arrested you because they're not sure you're the right guy to arrest."

"That's what I'm hoping. And I also think Jeremy is down here because he and his father can't figure out the delay. They must be getting nervous."

"They're not the only ones. You know what your father has been doing, right?"

Mitch nodded. "He gloats every night. And my mother has destroyed her efficient schedule and randomly sends people to the Sloane house to set up for the party and over to the construction office to get more float supplies, so they pretty much have no privacy."

Kristen laughed. "I know it's not funny, but I almost feel sorry for them."

Mitch gave her a look.

Oops. "But I'm over that now. Jeremy and his parents deserve to suffer."

Mitch checked his e-mail again. "I can't believe I haven't heard from him yet."

"Because…?"

"You'll love this." Mitch appeared smugly proud of himself. "So I log in and I find out that Jeremy has changed his password and there's an encryption program on my files. Remember, we're talking about a guy who has used the same password since college. Obviously, someone has been helping him and I hope it wasn't our IT guy, because it was a sloppy job."

"Fortunately for you."

"Yeah. Jeremy lacks finesse with computers, which he will never admit. For example, he overwrites files and is real quick with the delete key. I set up a shadow drive for him that backs up his backups."

"I could use one of those," Kristen muttered, knowing she lacked a certain finesse, herself.

"I could install one for you," Mitch offered. "It's no biggie."

"That's okay. Go on."

"Well, whoever was helping Jeremy reset passwords and encrypt data didn't know to ask about a third back up system. He probably gave Jeremy a list of instructions, obviously assuming he knows more about computers than he does. Jeremy, being Jeremy, wasn't about to correct him. So, the shadow drive was never changed and I was able to get into the system. The files weren't the latest version, but they were close enough. Here's the good part."

He looked so gleeful that Kristen smiled.

"I switched drives and put in a macro so that when Jeremy logs in and tries to open certain files, code scrambles and he gets gibberish. And I locked him out of my files."

Okay. Okay, maybe she wasn't *quite* getting it. "Just so I can fully appreciate your brilliance...basically, Jeremy is stupid when it comes to computers—"

"Not *stupid* stupid."

"But stupid enough that he needed help to fix it so you couldn't access your company files anymore."

"Right."

"But he forgot that there was another copy of everything on a 'shadow drive.'" She made finger quotes.

"Or didn't think it mattered."

"So you sabotaged it and magically—" she wiggled her fingers "—switched it for the real one?"

"Magically?"

"You did all that without actually being on his computer?"

"Our files are stored on a network server," he explained.

Or thought he explained. "Uh..."

"Big central computer."

"Gotcha. So why will Jeremy contact you?"

"Because he always calls me when he has computer trouble. He doesn't want anyone else to know how inept he is. And when I help him, I'll see what he's got hidden on his laptop. They have to have the laundering records somewhere."

Mitch was so confident and all Kristen could think was that his plan hinged on Jeremy's pride. "Still, I can't believe even Jeremy would have the audacity to ask the man he's trying to—"

Mitch's hand buzzed. Or rather the phone in Mitch's hand buzzed. He checked the display and then triumphantly held it so Kristen could see.

Jeremy.

"What do you know," Kristen said.

They high-fived each other and Mitch answered the phone.

Chapter Eleven

Things began to move after Jeremy's phone call.

Up until then, Mitch had felt as though he'd contributed nothing to his own defense. Kristen and her parents—even Mitch's parents—had done more than he had.

After playing detective, his father had insisted on hiring a lawyer.

Mitch had been against it because he already *had* a lawyer to whom he paid a very nice fee, and now doubted Jeremy's conflict of interest explanation.

His father had listened to everything Mitch had said, and then announced, "I hate shopping, so when I find the perfect gift I buy it. I'm buying you a lawyer. Merry Christmas."

Even Mitch's mother, in the midst of parade frenzy, assembled a list of VIPs who would be in attendance at the kickoff party and gave it to Barbara to see if there were any hits on *her* list.

So basically, it was the Save Mitch project and he'd felt useless.

That was about to change.

But not before Kristen got a hold of him.

They were in his parent's bedroom because that's where the full-length mirror was. He could smell his mother's perfume and see his dad's suits lined up in the closet.

This was the opposite of an aphrodisiac.

"Let's go over this again."

"Kristen..."

"Mitch, you're playing a role and you need to practice so you'll be convincing."

"I'm playing me. Jeremy knows me."

She shook her head. Her forties-movie-star hair had frizzed during their lunch, and she hadn't reapplied her red lipstick, so in her black skirt and white blouse, she looked more like a strict school marm than a femme fatale and Mitch could go with that.

Or he could have gone with that if his parent's king-sized bed hadn't been visible behind him in the mirror.

"But you know what Jeremy has been doing. You have to play a Mitch who still doesn't suspect. Jeremy is going to be watching for any sign that you do. And I've got to tell you, if you give him one of your disgusted looks, he'll know."

She had a point. She had a very good point because it was so much more than disgust. "Okay."

She made him practice greeting Jeremy, rehearse a few conversational lines and craft an explanation of what he'd been doing with his time.

"Would you ask about your clients?"

"Yes. I'd be frantic about my clients."

"What kind of answer would you be willing to accept?"

"That they've been taken care of."

"Then if Jeremy's explanation is the least bit believable, you accept it. You express relief, gratitude and admiration."

"Admiration? No way." He would have inserted a certain crude adjective, but they were in his parents' bedroom, after all.

"Admiration," she reiterated, crossing her arms over her chest. She was utterly sure of herself and this was serious to her.

He should respect that. "Okay."

"Remember that Jeremy's ego is the key. Next step. You're at the computer. What's your explanation of the problem and how much are you going to fix?"

"I'll access the registry—"

Kristen held up a hand. "You don't have to tell me, but you have to know. If Jeremy doesn't leave you alone with his computer, then you'll have to distract him."

"How? Yell, 'Look, it's Santa Claus!' and download files when he runs to the window?"

"Think ego. What does he do better than you?"

Mitch remained silent.

"What does he *think* he does better than you?"

"People. Women."

"Then you tell him you've met someone. You act sappy. That'll also explain away any weirdness in your behavior. Now, show me sappy."

Mitch made kissing sounds and batted his eyes.

Kristen thwapped him on the arm. "You are going to thank me later. You will be down on your knees in gratitude. You will owe me. And I will collect."

A wave of affection washed over Mitch. He deliberately tamped down any desire, primarily because of the psychological unease of being in his parents' bedroom with a woman he desperately wanted. In every way.

He usually delayed getting physical in his relationships and to his surprise, more often than not, the woman complained or wondered what was wrong with her. Mitch wanted to get to know his bed partners before doing the deed—didn't they want to get to know him?

Sometimes, they didn't. And that was a deal breaker for him.

Mitch liked to let the initial fizz of attraction develop into something many sided, and certainly one of those sides was physical. He was well aware that it was time to work on the physical side with Kristen. Not that it would be work. But she deserved all his attention and all his emotional energy, and until he cleared his name, that wasn't possible.

His eyes skimmed her face because if they skimmed her body, he'd never be able to concentrate on her instructions.

"Excellent." Kristen was watching him in the mirror.

"What?" He'd zoned out for a moment.

"Your sappy look."

Mitch cleared his throat. "Okay, what next?"

"Describe her to Jeremy. He'll ask. In fact, use me. I'm perfect."

Mitch raised his eyebrows.

Still holding her arms above the elbows, she paced as she thought. "As soon as you say my name, he'll stop paying attention to what you're doing at his computer.

Think ego. He's jealous of you. You'll go on and on about me so he'll know you're really infatuated."

"No acting, there," Mitch said.

She broke off to give him a big smile and then stepped forward and raised her arms. She was going to kiss him. He stepped back before he could stop himself.

She halted, arms in midair. "You're totally creeped out by being in your parents' bedroom, aren't you?"

"Yes."

Kristen dropped her arms. "Completely understandable." She glanced at the bed. "Completely. Now, where were we?"

"How wonderful and fabulous you are."

"And hot. Don't forget that."

"I never do."

She grinned. "I bet Jeremy says something like, 'Is Kristen still as hot as she was?'"

"Jeremy's ego isn't the only one I wonder about."

"I'm not naturally hot. I have to work at it. Hot is a state of mind."

Mitch thought it was a state of body.

"The point is to make me seem like exactly the type of woman Jeremy would want to attract."

She *was* exactly Jeremy's type of woman.

"And my Miss Sweetest crown won't hurt. Remember distraction and ego. By this time, he'll be thinking about trying to get me away from you so he can finally feel he's the better man. This is where you feed his ego. You admit that you've never dated someone like me and you are unsure of yourself. Ask his advice, since he's had lots of experience. He'll have forgotten all about his computer."

Kristen had been pacing behind him as she came up with this little scenario. "Oh, oh!" She gestured wildly. "Tell him you hope your situation gets straightened out soon because a woman like me expects certain things and you haven't been able to afford those things."

She's right. And you've bought her exactly one delicious, but cheap, Mexican food dinner. Mitch gazed stonily at himself in the mirror.

"Wrong face."

He met her eyes directly.

"Mitch." She put her hands on either side of his face. "A woman *like* me. Not me."

He was kidding himself. What did he have to offer her?

"Do not insult me by arguing with me about this," she demanded fiercely.

"You deserve more."

"So do you. And you're going to get it. Now, from the top. I'm Jeremy and I've just let you in the house."

"SO HOW HAVE YOU BEEN keeping yourself busy?" Jeremy leaned against the massive wooden desk in the downstairs office that Mitch had seen through the window several days ago.

He studied Jeremy's open laptop. "My mom is a total stress bunny with all the parade stuff." He mentally apologized to his mother. "Dad and I are just her minions." He logged in using Jeremy's new password—which Jeremy had given to him after explaining that federal agents had insisted that he change everything. Yeah, right.

Garbage filled the screen. "Oh, I see. Have we got a server problem?"

"Uh, no."

Which told Mitch that Jeremy hadn't asked their IT guy to investigate. Good. "But no one else complained of having computer issues."

"Mmm." Actually, what Mitch really wanted to say was, "How could they when they're all on vacation because you closed the office for the holidays?"

But he didn't. Mitch had also forced himself to swallow Jeremy's claim that he'd had no trouble handling Mitch's clients and running the office as usual. He'd expressed admiration and Jeremy soaked it up.

So far, Jeremy had stuck to his side, watching everything Mitch did. Mitch let the laptop screen fill with garbage a few more times to make it look good. "Let me try my password." Mitch typed rapidly.

"Uh..." Jeremy rubbed the back of his neck.

PASSWORD NOT RECOGNIZED ACCESS DENIED

Mitch waited to hear what he'd say.

"There's some scrambling thing..."

"Encryption program?"

"Yeah."

Mitch kept his eyes on the laptop as he felt his anger grow. *Distraction and ego*, he heard in Kristen's voice. *Accept any plausible explanation.*

"Well, that's what's wrong." Mitch sat back and gestured to the screen. "The encryption is leaking over to your files. Encryption programs are really complicated and notoriously finicky. A typo has been known to set one off."

Somewhere, a computer geek was rolling in his grave.

"Can you fix it?"

Mitch rubbed the place between his eyes and checked his watch. "Yeah. It might take awhile."

"How long?"

"It could take minutes or it could take hours. First, I have to poke around and find the leak."

"Oh." Jeremy was visibly relieved. "So it's not like it's going to take days or anything."

"No." Mitch focused on the screen, hoping that Jeremy would leave him to it.

"What are you waiting for?" Jeremy hadn't moved.

Mitch studied his watch.

"Got a hot date?" Jeremy stopped just short of sneering.

"Actually…" Mitch smiled to himself. "I've met someone. Someone special." He looked up at Jeremy and let his face go sappy. It wasn't hard since he *had* met someone special.

"Mitch, you dog." Jeremy punched him in the shoulder. "So tell me about her."

Just as Kristen had predicted. "Well, she's sweet—"

"The ones from Sugar Land usually are." It was an old joke but Jeremy laughed as though no one had ever said it before. "So she's like an elementary school teacher? Church choir director?"

Women not flashy enough for Jeremy. "Actually, she's an actress."

Though he stared at the screen, Mitch could feel Jeremy's attention shift.

"Oh, a drama teacher."

"I don't think so." Mitch punched up the source code for Jeremy's monitor, which Jeremy wouldn't know, and it filled the screen nicely. "You might remember her from school—Kristen Zaleski?" Mitch looked up.

Jeremy literally froze. "Kristen Zaleski?"

"Yeah. Do you remember her?"

"The Miss Sweetest Kristen Zaleski? Hollywood Kristen Zaleski? Homecoming queen Kristen Zaleski?" Jeremy stared at him in stunned disbelief.

Was it *that* unbelievable?

"That's the one." It was sappy look time. "She's sweet and sexy and smart and fun to be with."

"I'll just bet she is." Jeremy dropped his head back and wandered around to the other side of the desk. "Dude, I can't believe you're hanging out with *Kristen Zaleski*." While Jeremy shook his head in amazement, Mitch took the chance to display the contents of his hard drive.

Jeremy flopped onto the leather side chair across the desk from Mitch. "Is she still just totally hot?"

"Incredibly hot." And incredibly smart where people were concerned. Jeremy was acting exactly the way she'd predicted. "Incandescently hot. Almost too hot, you know?"

"No," Jeremy answered. "No such thing."

"She's got a belly ring."

Jeremy moaned and closed his eyes. "Stop. You're killin' me."

Mitch not only didn't stop, he followed the rest of Kristen's advice, including asking Jeremy tips for impressing a woman like Kristen. At the same time, he copied bits of information he could retrieve later. He would have loved to dump the contents of Jeremy's hard drive into his own computer, but even Jeremy would catch that.

"Mitch. Buddy."

Mitch had to look up.

"Are you telling me that you haven't nailed her yet?"

His fingers slipped on the keyboard and his face warmed with the effort of restraining himself from reaching across the desk and strangling Jeremy.

Fortunately, Jeremy interpreted Mitch's reaction as embarrassment. "Don't feel bad, buddy. You're not used to handling that much woman."

I'm selective, not incapable, you condescending, pretentious… And what have we here? Encrypted spreadsheet files. Jeremy was neither the encryption nor the spreadsheet type, especially not on his personal laptop.

Mitch could stand a few insults if it bought him time. "So what do I do, Jer?" And then he met Jeremy's eyes and spoke from his heart. "I've never felt like this about anyone before."

Jeremy settled back, fingers laced behind his head, and swiveled back and forth in the chair. "A woman like Kristen will expect you to take charge. And nice guys aren't going to turn her on, if you know what I mean."

Jerk. Mitch tuned him out and tried to access the files. Not happening. He'd need password retrieval software which he didn't have and which the FBI did. Kristen's father might have something, though. Mitch was going to have to get access to Jeremy's computer again, but if he didn't fix it now, Jeremy might take it to whoever had helped him in the past and Mitch's little nuisance programs would be discovered. Then the bad guys would know Mitch suspected them, so he had to remove the programs now.

There wasn't much more he could do here, anyway.

"Have you even been listening?" Jeremy had stopped relating hints designed to demonstrate his sexual prowess.

"I think I've found what I was looking for."

"Mitch, buddy, you were paying more attention to a computer than to me? Dude, that was my best stuff. I don't give that out to just anybody. No wonder you can't get a woman."

"I have a woman." Mitch typed in a few keystrokes. "A lot of what you said was just style. You have yours and I have mine. I think Kristen will prefer mine." He met Jeremy's eyes in a direct challenge and turned the laptop around to face him. "All fixed."

"HE ASKED IF I was still hot, didn't he?"

Kristen was deservedly smug.

"Yes." They were in the Noir Blanc offices waiting for Mitch's dad to arrive.

"So what did you tell him?"

Mitch leaned sideways and spoke through gritted teeth. "Not in front of the parents."

She beamed at him. "That hot, huh?"

Mitch was not entirely happy with the situation here. In addition to his mother and Kristen's parents, Carl Zaleski had brought in a policeman friend of his who was currently one of the area's Santa Claus security. He was dressed as the jolly old elf himself, although he'd temporarily removed his hat and beard.

Mitch had protested vehemently, but had been

outvoted. Since when had this become a voting issue? But the Santa cop was there to provide a record that Mitch had contacted authorities as soon as he had any evidence to back his suspicions, and to make sure that evidence would remain admissible in court.

The door opened and he smiled at his father, the smile fading when he saw that he'd brought a man with him.

Why not just announce Mitch's FBI problem to the entire town?

"This is Wayne Halloran, Mitch's attorney."

"Dad—"

"And Christmas present. See? There's Santa."

The laughter broke the tension in the room. Kristen's father stood and met Mitch's eyes in a reassuring look that also asked for Mitch's trust.

And he was prepared to wait until he got it.

Mitch gave him the slightest of nods.

"In the course of gathering information for my client, we discovered a situation…"

Somehow, Carl Zaleski laid everything on the table without making Mitch appear stupid, for which he had Mitch's gratitude and admiration—the real things.

Mitch added the pieces of information he'd gleaned from Jeremy's hard drive. "I want the opportunity to try and decrypt those files."

His lawyer, the cop and Carl all shook their heads. "It would take you several lifetimes with current technology," Carl told him. "You'd need the password."

Mitch smiled. "I think I have it."

"How?" Kristen asked as everyone stared at him.

"I found it in a file named 'file access.'"

"You're kidding," Santa cop said.

Mitch shook his head. "It's typical Jeremy. But I want to go back and try the password and see what happens and I don't want him there when I do it."

"Do it during the kickoff party at the Sloanes' house," Kristen said. "We'll keep Jeremy busy and you can sneak in then."

Mitch's lawyer spoke up. "I'll remind everyone that my client has a business partnership with Jeremy Sloane and that Mr. Sloane has requested my client's assistance and was granted access to both domicile and computer, which establishes previous—"

"He's covered," Santa cop interrupted.

"Is this an official—"

"I said he's covered."

This was one Santa Mitch wouldn't want to meet in a dark chimney.

"I want to hear what Kristen's got in mind," Patsy said.

"Okay. Here's what I'm thinking." She tossed him a smile before continuing.

Mitch sat back. For the first time he didn't just hope he'd get out of this mess; he believed it.

THE NEXT TWO DAYS were crazy because Kristen was preparing for the performance of her life.

As part of the evening's entertainment at the annual Christmas Light Parade Volunteer Appreciation kickoff party, Kristen Zaleski, former Miss Sweetest, and rising Hollywood actress—never mind the details, it sounded good—had graciously agreed to sing a medley of Christmas songs.

And allow Jeremy Sloane to try and seduce her, but that wasn't on the program.

Mitch, showing a real knack, had set up the situation perfectly. The rest was up to Kristen. All she had to do was become the woman every man wanted that night and that called for the heavy artillery.

She needed a dress and not just any dress. A classy, sexy, red dress that would make men drool and their women grudgingly not blame them. Nothing trashy or tacky or over-the-top sparkly, and nothing showing too much skin.

Which is what she'd just finished explaining to her former pageant dress seamstress, Teresa Nguyen.

"I got it," Teresa said. And Kristen knew she did.

Checking inventory on her computer, Teresa climbed on the ladder behind her and brought down a shoebox without Kristen asking.

"You wear these." After setting them on the counter, Teresa disappeared behind a curtained doorway.

Kristen tried on the white satin strappy sandals because no one argued with Teresa. Or at least winners didn't.

Teresa returned carrying a bolt of red satin charmeuse with a muted sheen that gave it a rich look. "We dye the shoes to match."

Kristen stood and instantly became four inches taller. She was not going to be walking far in these shoes.

Teresa took an electronic gun and zapped the fabric, typed in a command and waited. "Okay." She gestured to Kristen. "Here is your dress in that exact color."

Kristen looked at the monitor. "There's my dress." The style Teresa had chosen was a fitted, strapless column that fell to the floor. It revealed everything while revealing nothing and it was exactly what Kristen had wanted without knowing it. "Teresa, you're a genius."

"Yes. Now, I take your measurements."

"You have my measurements on file."

"Old measurements." Was Teresa staring at her stomach?

Kristen meekly followed her into the back dressing area and submitted to another measuring.

"You need hair," Teresa pronounced.

"I have hair." She kept it just below shoulder length for versatility.

"More hair. Get it. With this dress, you don't wear jewelry. No earrings, no necklace. Hair."

And so, between getting hair extensions and rehearsing with the band, Kristen didn't get to see Mitch until a few hours before the party.

"Is this *really* necessary?" Mitch glared at his reflection as Kristen's stylist added blond foils to his hair.

"Yes. Why are you arguing with me?" She hadn't argued with Teresa. "Don't you recognize genius?"

"I recognize genius, but I'm not going to recognize myself."

"That's the point!" Kristen looked heavenward. "We don't want anyone to recognize you. Your mother will tell everyone you're running an errand for her. And if Jeremy thinks you're off busy with the parade, then he'll feel free to go after me."

"He'd go after you anyway."

"True."

Mitch chuckled softly.

"You know he would! He'd do it to get to you. But even Jeremy would find it a challenge to convince me to ditch you for him while you're standing right there. So he'll be watching you and waiting. And if he has any kind of success with me, he'll want to see if you notice. You don't want Jeremy watching you. Therefore, the Mitch he knows will not be there."

Mitch scratched his face, where he was growing some nice stubble. "You think this will work?"

Kristen smiled. "If it doesn't, it will be because you will fall under my spell and forget what you're supposed to be doing. Ignore me. Don't listen, and for heaven sakes don't look."

"MOOOOOM! HELP!" Kristen collapsed onto her bed in exhausted defeat.

Barbara hurried in. "You're not dressed yet! It's time to leave."

"I want to make a grand entrance," Kristen mumbled.

"That's not going to give you the effect you want," her mother said.

"I can't get this thing on." She tugged and kicked her feet in frustration. "And this Rapunzel hair keeps getting all tangled in stuff."

Barbara chuckled. "What is that?"

"It's a body shaper."

"Your knees don't need that much shaping."

"That's as far as I can pull it up." She looked pleadingly at her mother. "Help?"

Clearly amused, Barbara brushed aside the lengthy strands of hair. "Stand up." She walked behind Kristen and tugged and with Kristen pulling from the front she finally squeezed herself into the shaper. She was out of breath and beginning to sweat.

Fanning herself with her hand, she asked, "How

could you ever stand to wear a girdle? How could you even get into one?"

After a disgusted snort, Barbara answered, "My generation was smart enough to get rid of those things. You'll have to ask your grandmother. Need help with your dress?"

Kristen slipped on her red sandals, stepped into the dress and her mother zipped it. Okay. The struggle was worth it. Kristen turned to the side and admired her flat stomach. Once she arranged her hair, look out Mitch. Except it was supposed to be look out Jeremy, but it wouldn't hurt to tweak Mitch, too.

Eyeing her daughter, Barbara said, "I hope the women of Sugar Land are still speaking to me tomorrow."

"MITCH, YOUR OWN MOTHER wouldn't recognize you and since I am your own mother, I speak on good authority." And then Patsy looked away. "I can*not* look you in the eyes."

Mitch wore blue contacts. Even he had trouble looking at himself.

"Good luck." His father patted him on the shoulder. "We'll see you there, but pretend not to."

Mitch gave them a lengthy head start and then followed in their SUV.

So this was it. The big holiday bash thanking the parade volunteers and kicking off the annual Christmas Light Parade. No doubt it was also Mitch's only chance to salvage his personal and professional reputation and avoid jail time.

No pressure, or anything.

Clearly the entire city had figured out a way to get

invited to the party at the Sloane residence because it would be the only opportunity most people would ever have to see the interior.

When Mitch had been in school, the kickoff party had been hot chocolate and Christmas cookies in the high school gym and the only volunteers had been the parents of the students in the parade.

Now, Santa Claus–costumed police directed cars to the nearby golf club parking lot. People were ferried to the party in a fleet of golf carts.

Thinking about the night ahead, Mitch failed to notice that the group of girls sitting across from him had been checking him out until one nudged his boot-clad foot.

"You from Sugar Land?"

"I grew up here." He looked up and met a gaze of frank interest. He blinked and noticed three other gazes of frank interest, the kind of frank interest usually directed at Jeremy.

Hot is a state of mind.

Kristen had rehearsed him on this character she'd created. Something about maintaining an aloof manly confidence. His expression was supposed to convey "We both know I'm hot. What are you going to do about it?"

Sounded like Jeremy to him, but she'd insisted that Jeremy lacked the essential aloofness.

"Do you still live here?"

He smiled slightly and paused. The pause was supposed to be important. "I'm visiting my parents for the holidays." He turned to watch their approach to the Sloane estate, aware of the looks the girls exchanged with each other.

The place was lit up inside and out. At least he wouldn't have to skulk around in the dark.

The cart stopped at the front entrance. Great. Now Mitch had to remember the walk that went with this look. An ambling stride. This look was very contradictory.

He must have succeeded because he heard the whispers and giggles behind him.

Either that, or they were admiring the fit of his new two-hundred dollar jeans.

He admired it, too.

Mitch walked his ambling stride up the steps and into the noisy crowd. Everyone was in high spirits in anticipation of the parade, and a constant stream of people flowed through the spacious living areas.

Mitch had never seen so many Christmas sweaters, vests and reindeer ties in his life. He actually felt conspicuous in his black leather jacket and cream cashmere sweater.

He saw Kristen immediately, or rather Kristen the Christmas Vixen every man wanted to find under his tree.

She was easy to find, since a news crew had camera lights trained on her. She…glowed. Glowed, that was it. On one side of her stood the mayor of Sugar Land and on the other a man who, if he wasn't the handsome governor of Texas, looked a whole lot like him. There were other men around her, men who eschewed flashy holiday garb for suits and a red or green tie. Behind them, more men waited for their turn to orbit Kristen. And behind them were determinedly smiling women who pretended not to notice.

How could anyone not notice?

Mitch swallowed. It didn't do any good. Her hair… her dress… That wasn't a dress. It was a couple of coats of red paint.

She'd warned him not to look. Good advice. He wrenched his gaze away from her and strode from the room. To hell with ambling.

He drew a shaky breath as he made his way through the foyer and into the other wing of the house.

She was acting. He knew that. But she was such a very good, very effective actress.

And of all the rich and powerful men surrounding her, Mitch was the only one who'd kissed her. Several times. His lips curled in a smug satisfaction and for once, he understood what drove Jeremy.

Jeremy.

Focus. He needed to focus.

There were more people spilling over into the hallways and the other ground floor rooms than Mitch had anticipated. He headed toward the office and got a sinking feeling as he heard laughter and voices. A group of older teens lounged on the chairs and sofa and flirted with each other, barely noticing him. Jeremy's laptop wasn't in the room.

Both good and bad, Mitch thought. It was probably in his bedroom upstairs.

Mitch returned to the main party room so Kristen would know he was there.

He circled the room, aware that he attracted some admiring female notice, which he acknowledged with a distracted smile.

And all the time he watched Kristen and the people

who watched her. And the man handing her a punch cup of wassail.

Jeremy.

Mitch got his own wassail and studied their body language. He didn't have to hear what Jeremy was saying—he'd heard it all before.

He smiled as Kristen gave him a working demonstration of aloof acknowledgement, which made Jeremy even keener.

He was really pouring it on and Kristen's reaction was nothing more than polite disinterest. She even let her gaze wander around the room while Jeremy talked, as though searching for someone more interesting.

That was harsh, but beyond effective.

And then her gaze landed on Mitch. He gave her his very best "We both know I'm hot" look and watched her hide her smile behind her wassail cup.

Though Mitch couldn't tell how she moved, her body language subtly changed and she sent him a sizzling look across the crowded room.

Jeremy noticed, as he was meant to, and turned to see who could have possibly stolen her attention away from him.

Mitch's heart kicked up a notch, but he leaned against the doorjamb and kept his gaze on Kristen.

Moments later, Kristen said something to the group she was with and went over to the band. That was Mitch's cue to leave, but a shift in the crowd alerted him that Jeremy was headed his way.

Instinct told him to stand pat.

Jeremy casually refilled his punch cup and, just as casually, came to stand next to Mitch. They both watched as Kristen approached the microphone and Mitch's mother announced the "special treat" and introduced her.

Amid enthusiastic applause and wolf whistles, the lights dimmed and Kristen picked up the microphone. There was a hushed expectancy just before she spoke to the crowd about how good it was to be back in Sugar Land.

"You know her?" Jeremy asked.

Oh, great. Mitch deepened his voice and answered in a raspy whisper. "Not as well as I'd like to."

"We're old friends."

Mitch glanced down at him and away. "Maybe she could use a new friend."

Bouncy music started and Kristen began to sing about rockin' 'round the Christmas tree.

Jeremy tossed back his wassail and set his cup on a tray. "Not while I'm roasting my chestnuts on her open fire."

"That's guaranteed to have her laughing all the way," Mitch said.

Jeremy looked him in the eyes so long; Mitch was convinced he'd been recognized. And then, without a backward glance, Jeremy made his way toward the bandstand, greeting people along the way, and arriving in time to applaud the end of Kristen's first song.

Jeremy hadn't known who he was after all. It fit, because Mitch clearly hadn't known Jeremy.

He should go find that computer. As he set his cup down, Kristen's next song started and she began a slow, bluesy, sensual version of *All I Want for Christmas*.

Mitch couldn't make himself leave. Around him,

men's jaws went slack while women gritted their teeth in envy. Even the catering staff stopped moving through the crowd and watched the woman in red.

And when she sang directly to him, Mitch broke out in a sweat. It was just a dress. It was just hair.

It was mostly Kristen.

For a few charged moments, they were alone in the room. Mitch could have stood there forever, but Kristen turned her attention to Jeremy. Mitch got the message.

It was now or never.

Chapter Twelve

Kristen had always known the power of perception. It was amazing how people could define themselves with the right props and the right attitude.

It was amazing how people never thought to look past the props and attitude.

The Sloanes, in their roles as generous community benefactors, had welcomed her as though she were visiting royalty. Whispers trying to guess the designer of her dress followed her through the crowd. More than one woman touched her own jeweled neck thoughtfully after taking in Kristen's spare elegance.

She even outshone the current Miss Sweetest, who stood in the VIP receiving line in her white cotton-candy-like dress, long white gloves, and sparkling crown, necklace and earrings. She looked overdone, while Kristen wore an air of Hollywood glamour and sophistication which was as fake as Chuck Sloane's integrity.

And then there was Mitch. As Kristen took the stage, she saw him watching her from the back of the room. Her mouth went dry and it was hard to swallow—not good before a singing performance.

And then Jeremy headed straight for him. How had he recognized him? While it was true that all Mitch had changed was his hair style and color, beard and eye color, it was his attitude that made him look completely different. He carried himself differently and when people reacted to him, he settled into his role.

Mitch didn't have an arrogant bone in his body. He was a good-looking man, but he didn't depend on his looks. What Kristen had done was bring out his Rocky Road side, something she doubted Jeremy had ever seen.

Still, she was rattled enough that she spoke a few words to the audience to settle her voice before she began to sing.

She didn't fully get into her song until Jeremy walked away from Mitch.

Her second number was designed to ensnare Jeremy, but she couldn't resist singing a little to Mitch, especially the "all I want for Christmas is you" part.

She couldn't be a whole lot more direct than that while still wearing clothing.

It gave her a thrill that he'd stayed to see her sing her sexy Christmas number. Even though accessing Jeremy's computer tonight might help him clear his name, even with that much at stake, he lingered.

How could she not fall in love with a man like that?

And because she *had* fallen in love with a man like that, she reluctantly sought Jeremy's admiring gaze and bent toward him. He looked her up and down as though she was a horse he was considering for purchase.

Countless casting calls had hardened her to such

looks and she didn't have any trouble giving him one right back.

He blinked a couple of times and Kristen turned it down a notch. She sang to some more men and returned to Jeremy, counting on his pride at having been singled out twice in front of the entire room to drive him to try to win her.

And *that* should keep him occupied until Mitch gave her the all clear.

THE PASSWORD WORKED, but Mitch almost wished it hadn't.

It had revealed a hidden operating system on Jeremy's laptop, undetectable except to those who knew it was there. A computer within a computer, like the false bottom in a suitcase. Kristen's father had suggested Mitch might find something like it, but Mitch was still startled when it booted up.

Obviously, Jeremy hadn't installed it himself, but he sure knew it was there.

Grimly, Mitch examined the contents. It was almost anticlimactic when he found the alternate accounting records. His name was all over them. Whether these were the real laundering records didn't matter—they looked like it and there was probably enough truth to them to satisfy the FBI.

Mitch connected to the Internet and sent a copy of the hidden drive's list of contents to his computer. Next, he copied the financial records and sent those.

A few minutes passed. Enough time for him to begin to think. He didn't want to think, so he poked through a few text files and found copies of e-mails between

Jeremy and his father in which an impatient Jeremy wondered what was taking so long and his father set up a meeting with the FBI in Houston so Jeremy could present "new evidence."

Mitch had no idea how long he stared at the screen as every possible explanation, every excuse and every hope that Jeremy had been as much a victim as Mitch died.

The Jeremy he thought he'd known better than any man on earth had never existed. Once Mitch accepted that, he could stop staring at the screen and function again.

He stuck his head out the bedroom door. Kristen was still singing, so he started transferring the entire hidden drive. He'd get what he could.

Mitch left the door open a crack so he could hear Kristen and sat on the floor. He could barely hear her, though.

He stared at the laptop on the credenza. It wasn't that he hadn't believed Kristen and her father, but seeing it all there on Jeremy's computer and knowing that Jeremy had played him for at least five years—and maybe from the beginning—hurt. Hurt on a level that was so deep, it affected the core of who he was. Seeing evidence that Jeremy not only was letting him take the blame, but was orchestrating it so he would, had changed Mitch. Sure, life would go on and he'd get past this, but he could never go back to exactly the person he had been.

He no longer trusted his judgment. Who else had fooled him? And for how long?

Applause sounded and the music started again. Kristen was leading a Christmas sing-along.

He closed his eyes and leaned his head against the wall. Tonight, every man in that room wanted her, including Mitch. His jaw ached from clenching his teeth. He loved her.

But did he know her? Who was she? She'd been playing one role or another the entire time they'd been together.

She acted as though she cared about him—but was that all it was? An act?

He needed to think.

Heedless of how much data he'd transferred, Mitch disconnected the laptop, put it back on the nightstand and walked down the stairs.

At the foot of the stairs, he could hear the applause as Kristen told everyone good night and to enjoy the parade. She'd be looking for him.

He couldn't. Not until he got things straight in his head.

So instead of returning to the main party room, Mitch walked out the back door and into the multicolored night.

WHERE WAS HE? KRISTEN had stalled, she'd vamped, she'd thoroughly alienated Miss Sweetest, and still Mitch hadn't reappeared.

She absolutely could not stay on the stage a moment longer.

She could, however keep Jeremy from leaving.

After leaving the stage, Kristen paid so much attention to him that his parents probably wondered if they should make an engagement announcement.

Jeremy was intent on making sure all the men

noticed that he was walking off with the prize female. He was so puffed up that if she'd poked him with a pin, he would have collapsed like one of the float balloons.

Kristen endured it for as long as she could, but it was hard to remain in character when the soles of her feet burned and the sexy straps on her sandals cut into her little toes. People were leaving to stake out their spots for the parade, anyway.

"I know a place where we can watch the parade in private." Jeremy's hand lowered to her hip.

Kristen adroitly moved out of reach. "I'm meeting someone," she said, making sure to add regret to her voice.

Something ugly flared in his eyes. "No, you're not."

She'd expected him to be difficult after all the time she'd been forced to spend with him. "Well…" She traced the knot in his tie. "Not without making a cell phone call first, I'm not. He's the son of my parents' friends. One must be diplomatic."

"One can use my cell phone." Jeremy produced it instantly.

"Then caller ID would ruin one's excuse." She wiggled her fingers. "I left mine in the car."

"I'll come with you."

"Which will result in an awkward encounter with my parents who are waiting for me by the door." Kristen held up a finger to indicate that they should stick around for her. "You're wasting time," she whispered. Turning, she gave him a look of sensual promise over her shoulder—too bad the promise wasn't for him—and walked toward her parents.

"Get me out of here," she said through gritted teeth.

Jeremy was only partly the reason. Her aching feet were the other part. Fortunately, their car was parked close to the house in VIP parking.

"What happened with Mitch?" asked her mother as soon as they were out of earshot.

"No idea. I stalled as long as I could."

"And longer," her father commented.

Kristen grimaced. "Was I awful?"

"He's just grumpy because he had to watch his daughter become the object of every man's sexual fantasy—"

"Barbara."

"Oh, Dad. Sorry. Ick." But then she smiled. "That must mean I was really good."

"You were fabulous!"

"For the *first* twenty minutes."

"Carl."

"Believe me, I so didn't want to lead a sing-along." Kristen moaned. "I sang *Grandma Got Run Over by a Reindeer* in *public!*"

Her mother put a sympathetic arm around her waist. "I'm sure Mitch appreciates it."

"It would be nice to hear it from him," Kristen grumbled.

"I wonder if we should worry." Carl unlocked the car.

"I'm going to call him." Kristen eased into as near a sitting position as she could get and got her cell phone out of her purse.

She had to call him three times before he'd answer. "Are you all right?"

There was a hesitation during which time Kristen's heart skipped a beat. "I needed to get away. To think."

Her father hadn't started the car yet. "Ask him if he got—"

Kristen held up her hand. "What happened?"

"I found a hidden operating system with financial records and instructions to Jeremy for exactly how he was supposed to present this to the FBI on Monday."

"Oh, Mitch." *Hidden operating system* she mouthed to her father, who nodded. "Where are you?"

"Kristen…I shouldn't be around anybody right now."

An icy dread gripped her. She'd never heard him like this. "Mitch, tell me where you are."

"Goodbye, Kristen." He disconnected.

Kristen didn't bother calling him back because she knew he'd turn off his phone.

She looked up to find both parents watching her. "Jeremy is going to the FBI on Monday. Mitch sounds horrible and he wants to be alone."

"Which means he shouldn't be," her mother said.

"Any ideas where he is?" asked her father.

"Not an idea." Kristen smiled. "A hunch."

PANTING, KRISTEN STOOD in front of the giant Santa Claus. The whole thing was covered in lights and he rotated while he waved with both arms. Surrounding him were various toys and a huge list with names that curled over the edge of the platform. The four-foot-tall boxy platform had been painted and covered with toys and lights that disguised the fact that there was room for an operator and machinery within. The float actually looked more spectacular from a distance because this close, she could see the wiring and construction details. But it was still impressive. And big. And bright. And hollow, which made it a pretty good place to hole up and think.

Kristen's breathing slowed as she recovered from running all the way from the far reaches of the mall parking lot.

Her parents had dropped her off at home where she'd peeled herself out of her dress and body shaper, changed into jeans and a red sweater with holly embroidered around the neck, driven like a mad woman on the side streets, and still managed to beat the parade here. Not by much, though. She could see the glow in the distance and faintly make out the drums from the marching bands.

The crowd was thick on the streets surrounding Town Square because people wanted to see the floats take their place in the Santa's workshop display. The only reason Kristen had been able to cross the barriers had been because Mitch's mother had stationed Nora Beckman at the end of the parade to direct them into place. Kristen told her Mitch was operating the Santa and she was bringing him something to eat.

And so now here she stood, shivering slightly as the wind picked up a little. She couldn't find the surveillance camera, but she knew there was one and she also knew Mitch could see her in all this light. She walked over to the door in the dollhouse, trying not to attract the attention of anyone but Mitch.

Looking up at the Santa, she held out a sack. "I come bearing grease."

Silence. Or rather silence other than crowd noise, a high school band playing *Deck the Halls*, generators, motors and a car horn or two.

Kristen waved the bag from side to side. "It's batter-fried fruitcake and it's still warm. Come on, Mitch. You want some. You know you do."

She could open the door herself, but she wanted him to. She'd come this far. He had to make the decision to talk with her or not. Holding up the other sack, she said, "Hot chocolate to wash it down. My hands are full. Please open the door."

She waited and was prepared to wait a very long while, but was glad she didn't have to as the door to the dollhouse swung inward and Mitch ducked out.

Kristen had forgotten about the shorter, lighter hair. He'd removed his blue contacts, though, and regarded her with dark, pain-filled eyes.

She should have brought tequila.

"So what role are you playing now?"

Kristen actually took a step back at the venom in his voice. Talk about misdirected anger.

"I'm debuting the role of the concerned girlfriend who brings her boyfriend fried fruitcake."

"Why?"

"A question I asked myself as I bought it. And you know what the answer is?"

He shook his head.

"Why not?"

Not even a smile.

"May I come in?" she asked.

Again, he shook his head.

"Even if I leave the fruitcake outside?"

"This isn't something you can tease me out of."

She knew that. "Remember how you owe me? I'm collecting."

His chest, encased in creamy soft cashmere, rose and fell. He ducked back inside. "Bring the fruitcake."

Smiling to herself, she followed him.

They had to bend over for a few feet while they walked beneath the platform, but when they reached the center, where an opening had been cut to allow easier access to the mechanics, they could stand up because they were actually inside the base of the hollow Santa Claus.

The lights shined through the thin skin. They were mostly the pinky red of the Santa statue and a multicolored glow from the pile of toys next to it.

"It's like being inside a kaleidoscope," Kristen whispered.

"I guess," Mitch allowed.

So he was going to be difficult. Looking around, Kristen saw the control area and the video monitors at one end beneath the toy pile. Mitch had been sitting on a folding chair and using the packing quilt for cushioning.

Kristen retrieved the quilt and spread it on the grass beneath the Santa Claus. Sitting, she patted the area beside her and set out the two cups of hot chocolate.

Mitch didn't move.

Kristen flattened one of the white paper bags and set the two cardboard sleeves containing the fried fruitcake on top.

Mitch didn't move.

She pried the lid off a cup of hot chocolate and took a sip. It had cooled to really warm. She swirled it around to mix the chocolate that had separated on the bottom and took another sip.

"Okay, Mitch." He stood slightly behind her and

she didn't turn her head. "This is my best shot. I've got nothing else."

The silence continued. Kristen couldn't begin to guess what he was thinking. He'd already known Jeremy and his father were guilty and, yes, that would take a while to get over. But why was Mitch shutting everyone out? Especially when they'd all worked so hard? Especially when *she'd* worked so hard?

"How can I get you to talk to me?" she mused aloud. After another sip of warm chocolate, she said, "I know. I'll tell you all about how I put up with Jeremy's insufferable arrogance and need for approval, his insolent remarks and crude suggestions, not to mention his wandering hands, for over an hour so you would be undisturbed. Or if that doesn't do it for you, think of your worried parents who had to leave the party early so they could get the parade started on time. Think of them wondering why they hadn't heard anything and if that meant you'd been caught."

Mitch sat heavily. Kristen had to grab his cup to keep it from falling over. She took the opportunity to mix up the cocoa a little.

"Jeremy was my friend," he began quietly. "I've been thinking about it and I genuinely believe he was my friend. And that makes what he's done worse."

Kristen took off the lid and handed him his chocolate.

He sipped it and went on, "We lived together. We went to school together. We studied together. We started our own business and lived together again until we could afford our own places. We knew each other as well as any two human beings can. He was the closest

I had to a brother. Yeah, I knew that he had faults, but so do I." He sipped at the chocolate again. "I know you told me what was going on, but I wanted to believe that Jeremy didn't know what he was doing. That maybe his father had forced him into it, somehow, or that it was an occasional thing." Staring at nothing, Mitch shook his head. "I thought I couldn't be that wrong about someone. But he's just evil. Accepting that changed me. I'm not the same person I was." He met her eyes. "I won't *ever* be that person again."

"That doesn't mean you're evil for trusting him."

"But it means my judgment of people is skewed. Why couldn't I sense that he's completely amoral?"

"He never showed that side to you. Think about it. You brought out the good in him because you expect people to be good. His father obviously brought out the bad in him. Jeremy is weak. He waits for others to define him. Their opinion of him becomes his opinion of himself."

Mitch didn't say anything, but Kristen could tell he was listening. "You expected him to be honest and aboveboard in his dealings with people, especially with you. To you, it's a given. That's the way you are. You certainly weren't going to say 'Jeremy, you were honest in this transaction. That's great. I really admire you for that.' But that constant praise is what he needs. I'm sure his father knows that and exploited it. Jeremy wants his father's approval. It's not too much of a leap to figure out what happened."

Kristen waited so Mitch could make the leap for himself.

And he did, as she'd known he would. "The extra

money bought him the cars and clothes and women to get even more approval."

"Yes."

"You're pretty good at analyzing people." Mitch swirled his cup.

"It helps me bring characters to life."

"For your acting." He swallowed the rest of the chocolate and replaced the lid.

"Yes." Kristen didn't bother finishing the rest of hers. It had gone cold. "I sense that you don't approve. Am I right?"

He turned his head and took in her jeans and sweater. "I've never seen you when you weren't acting. For all I know, you're acting now. Are you?"

"I'm acting that I'm not impatient with you. I'm acting as though it didn't hurt when you turned the anger you feel for Jeremy and yourself toward me. I'm acting as though I'm looking forward to trying that fruitcake."

She reached for it and took a big bite. The sweet crispy batter gave way to the still-warm interior, a rich mixture of candied fruit and nuts with a faint taste of brandy. "Mmm. This is wonderful!"

"And you're acting as though you enjoy that fruitcake, though I've seen better performances from you."

And then Mitch bit into his own fruitcake and surprise flashed over his face. "It *is* good."

Kristen nodded as she swallowed. "Whodathunk it?"

"See? I can't tell when you're acting and when you're not acting. I think I'm in love with you, but I don't know the you I'm in love with." And he took another bite of fruitcake.

Wait a minute. Back up. Had he…? Kristen mentally replayed his last comment. It sure sounded as though he'd told her he loved her, but instead of looking into her eyes and following up with a romantic kiss, he was eating fruitcake. "Did you just tell me you loved me?"

"Depends. Which Kristen are you?"

"All of them. And more you haven't met yet."

"That doesn't sound healthy."

"He says as he eats five thousand calories of fat."

"Which you brought to me."

"No one forced you to eat it."

He didn't respond. She was so not feeling the love.

"Mitch, you're an accountant who owns his own business. I've never seen your business. I've never seen you interacting with clients, but I know you. The financial stuff is what you *do*. It isn't who you *are*. But what you do does give insight into who you are. Acting is what I do. It isn't who I am. But my performances give you insight into who I am."

He'd been staring straight ahead, but now he shifted on the quilt until he could look directly into her eyes.

Kristen let him look and didn't try to express any particular emotion. Let him see that she was sincere, that she understood and sympathized, but that she had her limits. "Do you remember that first time at Noir Blanc?"

He nodded and she saw a faint smile.

"I told you who and exactly what I was. Do you remember what I said next? I said it was a relief not to have to pretend with you." She let that sink in. "And I never have."

"Tutti-fruitti," Mitch said.

"Oh, please. You weren't fooled. And you know why? Because you know me."

His gaze softened, but it wasn't with love. If Kristen was not mistaken, she saw regret.

"But you don't know me anymore. I've changed."

Bingo. Regret.

"We all change in some ways. I've changed, too. I thought I'd wasted the last six years of my life. I thought I'd failed at everything. I thought life had left me cynical and hardened. But it left me with insight and experience—and the ability to recognize a good person when I meet him."

"Isn't that the School of Hard Knocks?" he asked.

She smiled. "Guess so."

He smiled, too, but his faded quickly. "I…trusting…" He looked away. "I don't know."

"Okay, I'm not going to point out that trusting me is not the same as trusting people in the business world, but yes. It'll take you time to get over this. But you will. Mitch, you're an investor. When you invest, you expect a payoff. If your investment turns out to be a dud, you cut your losses and move on. You invested everything with Jeremy—business and personal. He's a dud and you feel you've lost everything. But you know something?" She scooted closer. "You'd started to diversify and you invested in me."

She wrapped her arms around him. "And I'm about to pay off big time."

She kissed him, their knee-to-knee position preventing any closer contact.

For now, it was enough. Kristen moved her mouth over his, the stubble scraping her chin enough to sensitize it and make this kiss different from any of their others.

He let her kiss him, but there wasn't much reciprocity going on. She pulled back, keeping her arms around his neck.

"Is this another attempt to restore my manhood?"

"If you'd quit losing it, I wouldn't have to keep helping you find it."

There went the half smile. "I thought you enjoyed the search."

"Oh, the searching is loads of fun, but I'm ready to find the pot of gold at the end of the rainbow."

"Wrong holiday."

She slid her arms from around his neck. "You know, all the build up to Christmas, the parties and the parade and the holiday food and the music, all heighten the anticipation, but eventually, Santa's got to come down that chimney."

Mitch's eyes had darkened and his breathing had picked up. He swallowed.

As direct as she could be while wearing clothes.

And still he sat there. She'd just have to be more direct, then. Kristen swept their food off the quilt, crossed her arms, grabbed the hem of her sweater and pulled it over her head.

She was wearing a red bra made of lace and very little else.

Mitch's lips had parted, his expression a battle between desire and restraint.

"Now, you can leave Santa milk and cookies, but I like to leave him these."

Bending backward so she could reach into her jeans

pocket, she withdrew a couple of condom packages and tossed them on the quilt.

Mitch stared at them and then met her eyes.

"So, hey, Santa," she said softly. "What do you say?"

He leaned forward onto his hands and crawled toward her. And kept crawling until she fell back onto the quilt and his arms and knees were on either side of her. "Ho, ho, ho," he said just before he kissed her.

He kissed her while running his hand along the length of her thigh, up her side, and along her inner arm. He kissed her while fisting his hands in her hair—hers and the fake stuff.

"Not good?" he asked when he felt her flinch. "Is it the beard?"

"The beard adds another sensation." She smiled and ran her fingers over his jaw. "But the thought of you coming away with a fistful of hair took me out of the moment a bit."

"Ah." He moved his hands to cup her face and his smile grew. "That was such a typical Kristen thing to say. I guess I know you after all."

"Not entirely." She looped her arms around his neck. "But I'm hoping we'll fix that soon."

She drew him to her, his head haloed by revolving pink lights. But when she thought he was going to kiss her lips, he bent and kissed her cleavage.

Surprise made her gasp.

"No? Yes?" he asked between kisses.

"Oh, by all means, carry on."

As though he'd needed an invitation. Mitch kissed her throat, her neck, and her eyelids. He licked her collarbone, her ear lobe and the top curve of one breast. The contrast between the mild scratching from his beard with the caressing softness of his sweater had her shivering.

"I—" Her breath caught as he tugged at her lower lip with his teeth. "I feel I'm not doing my fair share, here."

"You showed up. You brought condoms," he said roughly. "Trust me, that's more than enough." He kissed the crook of her elbow.

A very unsophisticated giggle escaped. "I—you're very…creative."

"I'm exploring you." His hand settled at her waist and his thumb caressed her skin. "I'm getting to know every part of you. I'm learning how you respond to my touch. I'm learning where you like to be touched. I'm learning how you like to be touched."

Her eyes widened. This was…this was…

Mitch parted her lips and delved deeply inside her mouth. Kristen heard herself moan. He'd drawn it out of her before she sensed it.

Taking his time, he drew back. "I'm learning how you taste." He drew his tongue just beneath her jaw and between her breasts. "I'm learning your scent."

He lowered his head and breathed in the crook of her neck. "And when I'm finished," he traced the shell of her ear with his tongue and lifted his head, "I'll know you anywhere, no matter what role you're playing or how you disguise yourself. And that's the you I'll love."

There were no words. But there were tears. Tears leaking from the outer corner of her eyes and into her ears.

Mitch tenderly wiped one away with his thumb and touched his tongue to the other.

Kristen shuddered. "No—no man has ever—" She swallowed.

"Made love to you?" His smile was tender with understanding, but his eyes were all self-assured, aroused male. "Then I'll be the first."

And he was. He absolutely was.

He made her feel. He made her think. He made her gasp and he made her moan. He reduced her vocabulary to repeating his name in gasping pants, long, drawn out sighs and pathetically grateful whimpers.

And then he undressed her.

Her vocabulary increased with the addition of "oh, yes" and "don't stop" and the occasional ragged "please."

And he was still dressed.

Propping himself on an elbow, he watched as she recovered from one of his "don't stops." He didn't bother to hide his smug smile, which ordinarily would have annoyed the heck out of her, except he really, truly—make that *truly*—deserved it.

Catching her breath, Kristen desperately tried to remember more words and managed a couple of small ones.

Lifting her limp noodle of an arm, she plucked at the extremely soft and utterly sensual cashmere sweater that she would never look at the same way again and said, "Off."

With the other arm, she pointed to the edge of the quilt where two square packages reflected the multicolored lights. "On."

Mitch stood and held her gaze as he methodically removed his clothes, stripping to Christmas carols.

The parade had reached the crowd gathered to watch

the display come together, and the bands had combined to play a concert of Christmas music.

Mitch stood looking down at her, his body bathed in the lights.

Kristen raised her arms. Mitch knelt and she drew him to her. "Please," she sighed. He captured the end of her sigh in his mouth and the gasp that followed when he eased into her.

She ran her hands over his back and as far down as she could reach, enjoying the novel sensation of his skin.

He broke their kiss to pull back until she could see into his eyes before he began to move.

He let her see his desire build, which fueled her own. She fought to keep her eyes open as the tension coiled within her until it was too much and she squeezed them shut, seeing the lights behind her eyelids as she peaked yet again. Quickly she opened her eyes to catch Mitch's heavy-lidded satisfaction at her pleasure before he buried his face against the side of her neck and shuddered his release.

They lay there, surrounded by lights and music and their own afterglow.

Being with Mitch had been the most incredible experience of Kristen's life. She'd been shocked at the depth of feeling and response he'd drawn from her. When their breathing had slowed and some of Kristen's brain function returned she had an awful thought. "Mitch?" she whispered, though with all the noise, he probably couldn't hear her.

"Hmm?"

"I...I think I forgot to tell you that I love you, too."

He gave her a lazy smile. “It’s nice to hear, but I already knew. Remember, I know you now.”

“Then you know I’m going to want my turn with you.”

Chapter Thirteen

Bright and early the following Monday morning, a number of people crowded a modest conference room in the Houston Field Office of the FBI. Present were three agents in the Asset/Forfeiture/Money Laundering Unit of the Criminal Investigative Division, a court reporter, four parents, one of whom was a private investigator, a lawyer, one girlfriend, playing the role of a modestly sweet innocent standing by her man and a scowling Santa Claus wearing a policeman's badge and an empty gun holster. Oh, and Mitch.

On the table was everything they'd found. Piles of papers. All Kristen's mom's suspicious real estate sales, Kristen's lists and chart—complete with salsa stains from their first date—and the information Mitch had gleaned from his company's server and Jeremy's laptop. The Santa cop was ready to swear that nothing had been illegally obtained, if it came to that. The lawyer was, well, Mitch hoped they wouldn't need him.

Kristen, who wore a dress with a white collar, low-heeled shoes, and had her hair—her really, really long hair—pulled back and fastened with a barrette, reached out and squeezed Mitch's hand.

"We're ready to begin whenever you are," said one of the agents.

Kristen's father was the appointed spokesman. He cleared his throat, but before he could speak, Mitch interrupted. "I need to say something here." He held up his hand to stop his lawyer from cautioning him. "What you are about to see makes me appear *unbelievably* stupid. I need you to keep an open mind and believe that I can be that stupid." He gestured to Carl. "Go ahead."

An hour passed and another. Mitch looked at Kristen and raised his eyebrows. Could she read their expressions?

She gave him a tight smile that told him she couldn't.

Finally, as hour three drew to a close, Carl Zaleski finished.

The three agents looked at one another and leaned together to confer. Expressions never changing, they straightened and faced Mitch.

Kristen laced her fingers through his.

"Okay." And that was it.

"Okay what?" Mitch asked.

"We believe you really were that stupid."

There was a shocked silence before the agents cracked smiles and everyone started breathing again.

Oh, and the blood returned to his fingers where Kristen had gripped them.

"Seriously," the senior man began. "Don't beat yourself up over this. You were used, not stupid. Honest people are predictable—they're always honest. Criminals like that kind of predictability. They count on it. As for the rest of this material—"

"Yes!" One of the junior agents fisted his hands and punched the air. "I weep for joy."

The senior guy nodded. "That about sums it up. Electronic funds transfers make these cases so complicated and difficult to understand. Juries get confused and frustrated."

"This is sweet." The junior guy unfolded Kristen's chart, the one she'd taped together to show the money trail to Mitch. The one with the salsa stains on it.

"Thank you," she said demurely.

The middle guy tapped Barbara's stack of material. "The real estate info." He made the "okay" sign with his fingers. "Prime."

Barbara inclined her head with a smile.

"Regular people came to the conclusion that something was wrong, so regular people in a jury ought to be able to understand why." The three agents stood as if by unspoken command, so everybody else stood, too. "Thank you for coming forward," the senior agent concluded.

"What about my furniture and car and bank accounts?" Mitch asked.

"We'll contact Dallas. They're not going to be able to release everything, but you ought to be able to get your bed back." He winked at Kristen who actually blushed.

As they left the conference room, they passed through the reception area and there, sitting on a leather sofa and holding his laptop, was Jeremy, there for *his* Monday appointment.

"Mr. Sloane, will you come this way please?" The senior agent was all business once more.

But Jeremy sat frozen to the sofa, his face going ashen.

Mitch walked forward until he stood directly in front of Jeremy, preventing him from standing. He could have yelled and threatened and called Jeremy names, but he didn't. It wasn't that he felt sorry for him; it was that he didn't want to waste any more emotional energy.

Looking Jeremy in the eyes, Mitch let him see the complete contempt he felt for him. "I'll have the receptionist water your plants."

Everyone but Kristen had filed into the hallway and were watching through the glass.

Mitch took a couple of steps toward them, but was brought up short when Kristen drew him to her, placed his hands on her bottom, drew her leg up and frenched him. Right in front of Jeremy.

Which was the point.

It was also right in front of assorted FBI personnel, their parents, a lawyer and an incredibly grumpy Santa Claus who wanted his gun back, but if Kristen didn't mind, Mitch sure didn't.

He had to help her make it look good, didn't he?

They made it look good just long enough to avoid having someone throw water on them.

"Oh, Mitch," Kristen said, and then appeared to remember her surroundings. Blushing charmingly—how did she do that?—she apologized prettily to the people in the office. "I love him so much I just forgot myself." Taking Mitch's hand, she led him out of the office.

At the last instant, Mitch looked back at Jeremy

being escorted down the hallway. He seemed shorter than Mitch remembered.

CHRISTMAS CAME AND WENT and Mitch came and went. He'd returned to Dallas to deal with the aftermath of Jeremy's money laundering scandal.

He called Kristen a few times and each time he sounded more tired and down.

Her father walked out of his office to the coffee pot. "So, Kristen, what are your plans?"

Talk about out of nowhere. "I don't know."

Carl glanced at her before filling a mug. "After that demonstration at the FBI—let me just say that again—the FBI—"

Kristen rolled her eyes. She'd explained about wounding Jeremy's ego, but would they let her forget it? No.

"—I thought you would be leaving with Mitch."

"I can see how you might think that." She'd thought that, too. "But I haven't been invited yet."

Carl sipped his coffee. "How long are you planning to wait for that invitation?"

As long as it takes. "I don't know."

"If you hadn't met Mitch, what would you do?"

"Build some savings and head for New York."

"Can't you wait for your invitation in New York?" he asked.

"Are you trying to get rid of me?"

"Yes."

Kristen gasped.

"Not that your mother and I don't love you, but you're just treading water here," he said gently. "You need to find what you were meant to do and do it. And if what you were meant to do doesn't earn you enough money to support yourself, then you find something that'll support both you and what you were meant to do."

"I was meant to be with Mitch." She sounded whiny and pathetic, not confident and grown up.

"Okay, you're meant to be with Mitch. Now what were you meant to *do*?"

She couldn't answer.

Staring into his coffee cup, Carl said, "After that incident at the FBI—"

Kristen rolled her eyes again.

"—I thought I was about to lose my receptionist. I hadn't bothered to hire one after the last one quit because I thought I could handle it all myself."

"You were kinda behind, Dad."

"I know. So, when I thought I was losing you, I offered the job to Nora Beckman. She starts next week."

She opened and closed her mouth. "You're firing me?"

"Uh…" He squinted. "I could be talked into some severance pay."

Kristen shook her head. "I've been mooching off you and Mom for weeks."

Her father smiled. "Your mooching license is still good. But I do have one other comment. It seems to me that a woman who kisses a man the way you did in front of the—"

"FBI. Yes, Dad."

"—is not the kind of woman who waits around for invitations."

MITCH CLOSED THE DOOR to seven years of his life without looking back. He gave his palms, which looked better now than they did when the FBI took them, to his neighbors, got in his car and drove straight to Sugar Land without stopping.

The Town Square Christmas decorations were to be removed on January 6th. Tomorrow. But before they were, Mitch had hired Sparky and The Electric Santa crew for the last job of the season.

FORTUNATELY, KRISTEN'S unemployment and Mitch's return to Sugar Land coincided.

They'd never talked about what would happen after the holidays and Kristen's chat with her father had shown her that she couldn't really make future plans until she knew if she was in *Mitch's* future plans.

His dinner invitation couldn't have come at a better time.

She thought a lot about what to wear and settled on a classic little black dress. Neutral. Appropriate for nearly any occasion.

Even dinner inside Santa Claus.

Mitch had asked her to meet him there. Kristen walked across the grass, now packed hard from days of being trampled. This time, when she knocked on the doll's house door, Mitch promptly opened it.

They stared at each other, neither making a move.

"Hey!" Kristen managed. "Your hair's brown again. But you kept the cut. I like it."

"Yeah." He ruffled the back of his head and ended up looking adorable.

He wore the new jeans and, if she were not mistaken, a cashmere sweater in blue.

She wanted to fall into his arms, but there was an

awkwardness that hadn't been between them before. And it was hard to do anything while walking beneath a four-foot ceiling.

When they reached the center, the outside lights came on, illuminating a blanket set for two.

"Something to drink?" Mitch asked. When she nodded, he poured an amber liquid into a wine glass.

Kristen sipped experimentally. "Wassail?"

Nodding, Mitch reached into an insulated bag and withdrew—

Two sausages on a stick, a dill pickle, popcorn, nachos and potato skins.

Kristen stared at her plate.

"And I have your favorite for dessert—fried fruitcake."

"Is there a message here?" she asked at last.

"It reminds me of you."

"I remind you of junk food?"

His smile was tender. "I will never drink wassail without thinking of you in the red dress. Sausage on a stick—the day you brought me lunch. Nachos—our first dinner. Popcorn—watching film noir movies after I saw you at your Dad's place."

"The pickle?"

"'We're the sweetest, you're so sour.'"

Kristen laughed. "Oh, no."

"Potato skins—exploring your skin."

"Oh, Mitch."

"And the fruitcake. That reminds me to try new things or to look at old things in new ways."

Kristen could hardly breathe as emotion choked her. "Mitch," she whispered. "You touched my heart."

"As you've touched mine." He took her hand and placed it on his chest. Beneath her fingers and the supremely soft sweater thudded his heart. "Come outside."

He went through the door first and drew her toward him as he backed away. Then he put his hands on her shoulders and turned her around.

The floats were dark and their lights were rearranged into a new display. The New York skyline outlined in lights stretched across the Sugar Land Town Square. Red hearts of all sizes pulsed and a multicolored "Marry Me, Kristen" flashed at her.

She stared and tried to figure out what it meant. Well, sure, she got the "marry me" part, but a "yes" hadn't bubbled up in response.

Mitch spoke quietly behind her. "I dissolved Sloane and Donner and closed the doors. I'm going to New York because I want to work in the financial center. I'm fruitcaking—looking at my old career in a different way and I'm trying something new."

Ah. He felt he owed her. Not so good. "Mitch, you didn't have to do this for me."

"I did it for me, but I didn't think you'd be all that torn up about joining me in New York."

So he was analyzing *her* now. And he was pretty good at it. His offer was so very tempting, but her father's words made sense. She needed to support herself. She needed to support her own dreams. "I—I don't want to use you just to support me while I try acting."

"Okay." Mitch was suspiciously agreeable. "I've already got an apartment with plenty of room, but you should get your own place, if that's what you want."

He already had—"How did you already find an apartment?"

"Through a client—a real one."

Kristen felt on the verge of something that could be wonderfully right, or horribly wrong. "I might not… well, I like acting, don't get me wrong. But I don't like everything about trying to get the opportunity to act. I enjoy creating characters by figuring out what makes people do what they do." Kristen was aware of the weight of Mitch's hands on her shoulders. "Before I dropped out of college, I really enjoyed psychology. In a big way."

"Go back to school, then."

"Again, I need to contribute financially."

"If you want to, but you don't have to."

"This is too easy. I don't get it."

Mitch laughed. "Kristen, you saved me."

"Not by myself."

"I'm not just referring to keeping me out of jail, although I do very much appreciate that. You saved me from the rut I'd been in. Everything was the same. I didn't have any joy anymore. I didn't even know what I was working for—I never spent much money because I didn't have time to."

Mitch folded his arms around her and pressed her back against his chest. "Even though it was bad worrying about what could happen to me, I didn't feel half as depressed as I did when I walked back into what was left of my old life." He inhaled and kissed the top of her head. "So I'm off to New York. For me. And I thought how lucky it was that you wanted to be there, too. But if you don't, then I guess I'll rack up a lot of frequent flyer miles."

"But I do! I do want to go to New York!" Kristen swiveled in his arms. "When? How much time do I have?"

"Anytime and as much as you want."

"Oh, Mitch!" She flung her arms around him and bounced little kisses off his chin and jaw and lips. "For the first time, I'm glad I have hardly anything to pack."

"So…you're coming with me?"

She pulled back. "Of course! I love you!"

This time she connected with his lips and held, kissing him with joy and excitement and pent up passion and love. The problem was that he wasn't kissing her back. "What's wrong?"

Mitch turned her around again. "Remember the time you forgot to tell me that you loved me?"

She smiled and nodded. "But you said you knew it anyway."

"I said it was nice to hear the words, anyway." He pointed to the flashing "Marry Me, Kristen" sign. "Forget something?"

She flung herself into his arms. "Yes!"

* * * * *

New York Times *bestselling author Linda Lael Miller is back with a new romance featuring the heartwarming McKettrick family from Silhouette Special Edition.*

SIERRA'S HOMECOMING
by Linda Lael Miller

On sale December 2006,
wherever books are sold.

Turn the page for a sneak preview!

Soft, smoky music poured into the room.

The next thing she knew, Sierra was in Travis's arms, close against that chest she'd admired earlier, and they were slow dancing.

Why didn't she pull away?

"Relax," he said. His breath was warm in her hair.

She giggled, more nervous than amused. What was the matter with her? She was attracted to Travis, had been from the first, and he was clearly attracted to her. They were both adults. Why not enjoy a little slow dancing in a ranch-house kitchen?

Because slow dancing led to other things. She took a step back and felt the counter flush against her lower back. Travis naturally came with her, since they were holding hands and he had one arm around her waist.

Simple physics.

Then he kissed her.

Physics again—this time, not so simple.

"Yikes," she said, when their mouths parted.

He grinned. "Nobody's ever said that after I kissed them."

She felt the heat and substance of his body pressed against hers. "It's going to happen, isn't it?" she heard herself whisper.

"Yep," Travis answered.

"But not tonight," Sierra said on a sigh.

"Probably not," Travis agreed.

"When, then?"

He chuckled, gave her a slow, nibbling kiss. "Tomorrow morning," he said. "After you drop Liam off at school."

"Isn't that…a little…soon?"

"Not soon enough," Travis answered, his voice husky. "Not nearly soon enough."

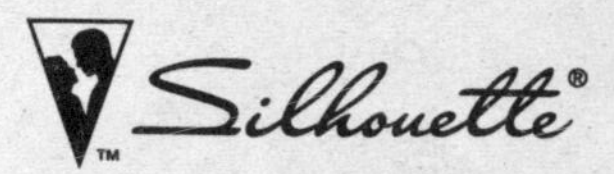

Romantic
SUSPENSE

INTIMATE MOMENTS™

Excitement, danger and passion guaranteed

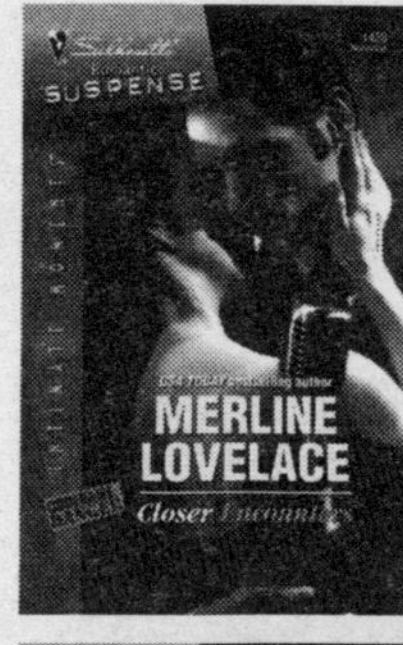

In February 2007
Silhouette Intimate Moments®
will become
Silhouette® Romantic Suspense.

Look for it wherever you buy books!

Visit Silhouette Books at www.eHarlequin.com SIMRS1106

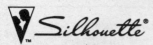

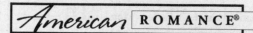

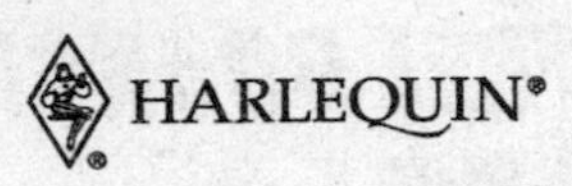

American ROMANCE®

COMING NEXT MONTH

#1141 A LARAMIE, TEXAS CHRISTMAS by Cathy Gillen Thacker
The McCabes: Next Generation
All Kevin McCabe wants for Christmas is to get closer to Noelle Kringle. She and her son are in Laramie for the holidays, and he finds himself strongly attracted to her. He can tell the feeling is mutual, but as quickly as Kevin's falling in love, he can't help but wonder what it is she's trying to hide.

#1142 TEMPTED BY A TEXAN by Mindy Neff
Texas Sweethearts
Becca Sue Ellsworth's prospects for cuddling a child of her own seem grim, until the night her old flame arrives first on the scene of a break-in to rescue her from a prowler. Suddenly she realizes she has another chance to get Colby Flynn to rethink his ambition to be a big-city lawyer—and to remind the long, tall Texan of a baby-making promise seven years ago…the one she'd gotten from him!

#1143 COWBOY VET by Pamela Britton
Jessie Monroe is the last person on earth Rand Sheppard wants to rely on, but he needs a veterinary technician—yesterday—and she's the only one for hire. It turns out the woman who destroyed his cousin's life isn't who Rand thought she was. And now she's all he can think about….

#1144 THE WEDDING SECRET by Michele Dunaway
American Beauties
After landing a plum position on the hottest talk show in the country, Cecile Duletsky is ready for just about anything. Anything but gorgeous Luke Shaw, that is. Cecile spends a fabulous night with him, knowing she isn't ready for a complicated romance. But that's before she shows up for work and finds Luke—her boss—sitting across from her in the boardroom.

www.eHarlequin.com

HARCNM1106